In the Penny Arcade

In the
Penny Arcade

STORIES BY

Steven Millhauser

ALFRED A. KNOPF   NEW YORK   1986

"A Protest Against the Sun" and "The Sledding Party" first appeared in *The New Yorker*; "Cathay," "Snowmen," and "A Day in the
Country" in *Grand Street*; "August Eschenburg" in *Antaeus*; and "In
the Penny Arcade" in *The Hudson Review*.

Library of Congress Cataloging-in-Publication Data

Millhauser, Steven.   In the penny arcade.

I. Title.
PS3563.I42215   1986   813'.54   85-40122
ISBN 0-394-54660-1

Manufactured in the United States of America

FIRST EDITION

To Cathy

Contents

PART I

August Eschenburg   3

PART II

A Protest Against the Sun   67
The Sledding Party   81
A Day in the Country   99

PART III

Snowmen   125
In the Penny Arcade   135
Cathay   147

I

August Eschenburg

YOUNG ESCHENBURG

At the age of eight, August Eschenburg spent long summer afternoons playing with a cruel and marvelous toy. It had appeared suddenly one day in the field down by the river, and it was to disappear just as suddenly, in the manner of all delights which reveal themselves too quickly and too completely. A hollow paper figure represented a clown, or a fireman, or a bearded professor. When you put a captured bird inside, the poor creature's desperate attempts at escape produced in the paper figure a series of wildly comic motions. August, who knew that the game was cruel, and who never told his father, tried more than once to keep away from the field by the river, but he always succumbed in the end. The other boys seemed to take pleasure in the struggles of the bird, but August was fascinated by the odd, funny grimaces of the tormented paper man, who suddenly seemed to come alive. This forbidden toy was far better than his music box with the slowly turning monkey on top, or his butter-churning maid who moved her arm up and down when you wound her up, or his windmill with sails that turned in a breeze. It was even better than his jointed yellow clown who all by himself could climb down the rungs of a little red ladder. August was relieved when school returned, and the cruel game in the field by the river disappeared as mysteriously as it had come, but he never forgot the sense of fear and wonder produced by those dangerously animated paper men.

He had always been fond of toys that moved, and for this love he considered his father in large part responsible. Joseph Eschenburg was a watchmaker by trade, and one of August's earliest memories was of his grave, mustached father removing from his vest pocket a shiny round watch and quietly opening the back to display the mysterious, overlapping wheels moving within. August could not follow the patient explanation, but he realized for the first time that the moving hands of a watch did not just happen that way but were controlled by the complicated wheels hidden away inside. Not long afterward, when his father took him to the North Sea and he saw waves for the first time, he was hurt by his father's gentle laugh when he asked whether the waves had wheels inside.

Young August was enchanted by the clocks and watches in his father's shop. He liked to step out of the busy street where it was always a certain time and enter a world where it was many times together and therefore, in a way, no time at all. He liked to open the glass doors of clocks that came in cases and to set the pendulum swinging with a finger, and he liked to hold the heavy pocket watches in the palm of his hand and feel the secret mechanism beating inside like the heart of a bird. He liked the gleaming porcelain clocks with their carved Cupids and shepherdesses, and he liked the clock dials that had scenes painted on them: a sunlit glade with dancing knights and ladies, a Japanese woman with a very white face and a very red fan, children skating on a pond with their scarves streaming out behind them. But most of all he liked the secret wheels within, which made the hands turn at different speeds and which formed a far more complicated and beautiful pattern than the carvings and paintings on the outside. From an early age he had begun to help his father in simple ways, such as carefully cleaning the tiny mechanisms that lay scattered on the worktable under the hot light, and soon he was learning to perform the less difficult kinds of repair. He learned that the secret of the motion lay in the coiled spring, which when it lay alone on the table looked terribly helpless and awkward and reminded him somehow of a dead fish floating in the water. He learned how the spring in its hollow barrel was made to coil tight when you wound the watch, and how it slowly unwound to turn the gear train, with its three wheels each turning more rapidly than the one before. The second of these three wheels moved eight times as fast as the first, making one revolution in an hour, and the third made one revolution every minute. This wheel was in turn geared to the escape wheel, and August learned to take apart and assemble the section composed of the escape wheel, the forked lever with its two tiny jewels, and the balance wheel with its hairspring. All these things his father patiently taught him, scolding him only when he was especially clumsy, and the time came when August was able to take apart a watch, lay out its precious contents on the table, and put all the pieces back together again. It was far, far better than his colored wooden puzzle called *Europe Dissected for the Instruction of Youth in Geography*. He understood that the same mechanism which turned the watch hands also drove the little men and women who on certain clocks would step stiffly forward and turn their heads from side to side, but those simple figures were of far less interest to him than the complex wheels themselves. Even the butter-churning maid that his father took apart for him failed to do more than satisfy his curiosity, perhaps because the motions of the toy could not equal the double wonder of minute hand and hour hand smoothly performing their flawless motions. Those motions were perfect and complete in themselves, whereas the motions of the clockwork buttermaid were a very imperfect copy of human ones. Much later, when his life had developed in a way that felt like a destiny, August was to think it strange that never once during his childhood had he attempted to construct a clockwork figure of his own, as if his considerable skill as a watchmaker existed somehow apart from everything else, awaiting a certain fateful jolt before it revealed its inner meaning.

August's mother had died when he was so young that he could scarcely remember her. Although his feeling for his mother was tender and reverent, she existed for him only in the little silhouette in the oval frame that his father kept on the night table beside his bed: a two-dimensional mother with a turned-up nose on one side and masses of curls on the other. For a while the boy had longed to penetrate that blackness, but later he was pleased that she had left behind only her shadow, as if his ardent, expansive feeling for her would have been unduly limited by too precise an image. But Joseph never forgave himself for failing to preserve his beloved Magda in a photograph—a mistake he was determined would not happen again. It was shortly after her death that the watchmaker first took little August to a photographer, and the child never ceased to marvel at the stern brown-and-white picture of himself in curls and knee-breeches, on a stiff cardboard backing. The new art of photography was scarcely a quarter of a century old, and much later, when the full meaning and destiny of the art were revealed to him, the early picture was to seem yet another fateful sign.

But far better than the cardboard photograph was the funny painting he saw one rainy Sunday afternoon in an obscure corner of the Stadtmuseum of a neighboring city, two hours by coach from Mühlenberg. He and his father had spent a long time admiring the splendid collection of clocks, the hall of doll-house miniatures, and the three rooms of early toys—wheeled horses from Berchtesgaden, flocks of lambs from Thüringen, goose-women from Sonnenberg—and August had begun to grow tired when with a mysterious air his father led him into the room of pictures. Pictures in museums looked all the same to August, and he was disappointed and irritable as he looked about at the faded landscapes showing little people here and there, and sometimes dogs, and ships on the horizon. He was relieved when his father did not make him stop in front of the pictures, but led him over to a guard in a dark green uniform, who smiled at August—how he hated that—and then stepped over to a picture which was not hung on the wall but stood upon a cabinet. The picture showed a castle and parks in the background, some gardens closer up, then a road with a wagon on it alongside a river with rowboats, and in the foreground some little people standing by the river with fishing poles in their hands. The thick frame, carved with fruits and flowers, seemed just as interesting, and the guard appeared to agree with him, for he raised his hand to the frame and seemed about to point. But instead he did something with his fingers, and then the strange thing happened: the wagon on the road began to move forward, the horse trotted along, the people in the row-boats began pulling their oars and the boats moved in the river, a fisherman in the foreground cast and slowly drew in his line, a laundress by the riverside began wringing out her clothes—he hardly knew where to look—and beyond the road, in the garden, two men bowed to a lady, who slowly curtsied in return, and far away in the castle park a man swung a croquet mallet and sent a little ball rolling along, while on the other side of the park some dogs chased each other out of sight.

He had guessed the secret of the magic picture at once, which in no way diminished its enchantment, and when the man in the uniform turned the picture around, August recognized the familiar wheels that controlled all the motions. The guard explained how the clock movement drove three endless chains, one for the river, one for the road, and one for the dogs. Two chains turned in one direction, the third in the other. All the other figures were moved by a system of levers worked by pins placed on the different wheels. August asked no questions, which seemed to disappoint his father, and the next day, in his room above the watchmaker's shop, when the twelve-year-old boy began to construct a moving picture of his own, it all seemed so clear to him that he marveled at not having invented such a splendid device himself. He worked obsessively on moving pictures for more than a year, inventing increasingly complex motions—his best picture showed a train moving through a forest, its wheels turning clearly while smoke poured from the stack, and the conductor waved his hat, and in the nick of time a sleepy cow stood up and left the track—but even as he passed from one success to the next he felt an inner impatience, a disappointment, an unappeased hunger, and one day he simply lost interest in moving pictures. He never returned to them.

It sometimes happens that way: Fate blunders into a blind alley, and to everyone's embarrassment must pick itself up and try again. History too was always blundering: the startling illusions of motion produced by Daguerre in his Diorama were in no way related to the history of the cinema, which was directly related to a simple toy illustrating the optical phenomenon known as persistence of vision. Yet perhaps they are not blunders at all, these false turnings, perhaps they are necessary developments in a pattern too complex to be grasped all at once. Or perhaps the truth was that there is no Fate, no pattern, nothing at all except a tired man looking back and forgetting everything but this and that detail which the very act of memory composes into a fate. Eschenburg, remembering his childhood, wondered whether Fate was merely a form of forgetfulness.

Indeed, trying to explain the particular shape of a life, one left out all sorts of things: the earthy smell of wet cobblestones, the glass-covered picture of the tall-masted ships in the harbor at Hamburg, the dull old schoolmaster in a chalky coat who, unlike all the others, turned out to be marvelously animated when it came to the one subject that really interested him: the multiplicity of leaf shapes, the miracle of diversity arranged by Nature in a single square kilometer of any forest.

Yet one had to admit that sometimes a moment came, after which nothing would ever be the same. On August's fourteenth birthday his father took him to the fair in the great meadow beyond the river. He had been to these fairs many times before, and each time they had filled him with wild excitement mixed with faint disappointment, as if a desire had been aroused without being satisfied. Now, at fourteen, with his voice already breaking, and shadows on both sides of his upper lip, he took it all in with a certain reserve: the booths where screaming hawkers displayed their hunting knives, their blood sausages, their green parrots, their jointed marionettes, their steins of foaming beer; the roped platform where a blubber-lipped Negro sat with a silver collar round his neck; the striped tents into which you were invited to step and see Elmo the Fire-Swallower, Heinrich the Learned Horse, the Hairy Lady of Borneo, Professor Schubart the Mesmerist, the Speaking Bust, the Automaton Chess-Player, Bill Swift the American Sharp-Shooter, Wanda the Ossified Girl, Count Cagliostro's Chamber of Horrors, Kristina the Captured Mermaid (A Lovely Natural Wonder), the Two-Headed Calf, Professor Corelli the Venetian Physiognomist. A woman with a red scarf tied round her head turned the handle of a hurdy-gurdy, a blind fiddler played beside a monkey on a rope, there was a smell of sausages and a sweet, hot odor as of boiling caramel. August felt restless and irritable. He envied the rougher boys his age who were allowed to prowl in groups without fathers, and he felt ashamed at being with his father and ashamed at feeling that way. A man with beer foam above his upper lip bent toward a fat-rumped woman in a feathered hat who threw back her head and laughed. August stopped at a booth offering knives and scissors for sale: there were long-bladed hunting knives whose carved handles emerged from fur-lined leather sheaths, bone-handled jackknives with the long blade out and the short blade at right angles, bread knives and butcher knives, knives for paring apples, mysterious knives with wriggly blades, thick knives with blades that sprang out at a secret touch—he could afford none of them. They wandered on, in the narrow lanes with booths on both sides. Hawkers shouted as if in rage; he felt spittle on his cheek. A dark green tent appeared, with a red streamer on top; above the open flap were the words KONRAD THE MAGICIAN. A tired woman in a turban sat on a stool, fanning herself with a folded newspaper. August had always been amused by magic tricks; his father paid the turbaned lady and they stepped inside.

It was dark and horribly hot. On a roped-off platform Konrad the Magician stood behind a table. On each side of him an oil lamp glowed. August saw at once that he had made a mistake: the magician was perspiring, the air was unbreathable, the crowd was composed mostly of children and mothers. Konrad was drawing from his fist a long stream of colorful silk scarves all knotted together; August had seen it a dozen times. If he was a magician, why didn't he make the air cool? Why didn't he turn the scarves into a mountain of gold, and take a steamship to America and live in a white house with pillars and a thousand slaves? Konrad came to the end of the scarves, crumpled them all up in his hand, shook his closed fist, and opened his hand to reveal a dead mouse, which he held up by the tail. The children laughed; August smiled wearily. Konrad wiped his sweating forehead with a black handkerchief. He next reached into his ear and removed a white billiard ball. He looked at it in surprise. Opening his mouth, he struggled to place the ball inside; slowly he closed his lips over it. He swallowed loudly and opened his mouth: the ball was gone. He leaned forward, showing his open mouth. Konrad closed his mouth, placed both hands on his stomach and pushed. Opening his mouth, he removed a red billiard ball. There was delighted laughter and applause. August, removing a watch from his pants pocket to glance at the time, discovered that he had not yet replaced the hour hand. The minute hand pointed to four. The time was twenty past nothing. Konrad removed the white billiard ball from his other ear, turned it into a pigeon, and picked up a curtained box which he placed on the table in front of him. He announced that he was going to shrink himself and appear in the box. August had never seen this trick and wondered faintly how he would manage it. Konrad took out his black handkerchief and mopped his brow. He shook the handkerchief, which became a white sheet. He held up the white sheet before him; a moment later the sheet fell lazily down, revealing empty air.

All eyes were now turned to the box on the table. The curtains slowly parted, revealing a dark stage, in the center of which stood a small table bearing an empty glass bowl. The table and bowl were brilliantly illuminated by three beams of light falling at angles from the ceiling. A music-box melody began to play. From the right wing emerged a shadowy man about the size of a nutcracker. He walked briskly to stage center directly behind the table and stood facing the crowd. He wore tails and a top hat and carried in one hand a black wand. His face was pale and his eyes were restless, dark, and bright. He stood motionless for a few moments and then rapped the glass bowl twice with the top of his wand, as if signaling for attention. He next held up the wand by one end and with his empty hand he pressed against the other end of the wand, slowly collapsing it until it was crushed between his small clasped palms. When he opened his hands there spilled out a bright white tablecloth, which he held up for inspection, turning it first one way and then the other. He laid the tablecloth carefully over the glass bowl, stepped back, and held up his hands for inspection. When he stepped forward and removed the tablecloth, the glass bowl was filled with water, and a little goldfish was swimming about. He bowed to the left and bowed to the right. Again he laid the cloth over the table, covering the bowl. When he lifted the cloth, the bowl was no longer there. He held up the tablecloth, turning it first one way and then the other. He bowed to the left and bowed to the right. He placed the tablecloth over the table. He removed his top hat and held it out for inspection. He shook it vigorously; he turned it topside up and topside down. He placed the black hat brim-down on the white tablecloth. When he suddenly lifted it, he revealed the bowl of water in which the little goldfish was swimming. He bowed to the left and bowed to the right. He put the top hat on his head. He picked up the bowl and he picked up the tablecloth. He set down the bowl and placed the tablecloth over it. When he lifted the tablecloth, the bowl was empty. He bowed to the left and bowed to the right. He held up the tablecloth for inspection, turning it first one way and then the other. He folded the tablecloth in half, and in half again, and in half again, until it was the size of a little handkerchief. He closed his hands over the folded bit of cloth and slowly drew forth the black wand. He bowed to the left and bowed to the right. Then turning on his heel he walked from the stage, exiting on the left. The lights dimmed and went out. Slowly the curtain fell. The whirring stopped.

Now the rumpled sheet lying on the stage began to flutter mysteriously, slowly it rose up ghostlike before the watchers, and from behind it stepped Konrad the Magician. He collapsed the sheet into a black handkerchief, mopped his brow, and placed the handkerchief in his pocket. Gracefully he bowed. The performance was over.

Never had August seen such an extraordinary toy. The tricks of the little magician had amused him, but far more fascinating was the little automaton itself. Although it was evident that he could perform only a fixed number of motions, the number was large and various enough not to fall into an ascertainable pattern, and the motions themselves were entirely without the fatal jerkiness of the tedious clockwork toys he had seen. True, there was a slight stiffness about the little clockwork magician, but that entirely suited his formal manner. Yet even more striking than the smooth and lifelike motions was the uncanny expressiveness of the magician's mobile face. He had moved his mouth and eyes, as well as his head, and August had seemed to catch a glimpse of cheek-muscle tightening. Indeed his face seemed so able to express the several emotions required of him that it was as if he were controlled not by an inner mechanism of wheels and levers but by a thinking mind; and it was above all this illusion of an inner spirit that was so remarkable in the performance of the clockwork magician.

To those few minutes in a drab green tent, August ever after traced his devotion to clockwork art. Even then he disdained the phrase "clockwork toy," for it was precisely those well-loved toys which had failed to strike a responsive chord in him. The clockwork magician was so far superior to the butter-churning maid that it seemed part of another world entirely, and it was that world and only that world which August longed for. Old Joseph encouraged the boy's new hobby, little suspecting he would never outgrow it. Together they made trips to toy shops in Mühlenberg, and in the winter evenings, after the last watch had been repaired for the day, August and his father took apart and reassembled automaton toys. The mechanisms were startlingly easy for him to grasp, but at first the automaton motions proved difficult to foresee, for he was used to transforming the intricate system of wheels and springs into the simple circular motions of clock hands. Even the mechanical pictures worked only in two dimensions, and now he had to think in three. Often he was angry at himself, as if he had wasted his life. But the toys were far simpler in structure than his beloved clocks and watches, and after a month of odd, irritating clumsiness everything seemed suddenly clear. He even began to introduce little improvements of various kinds: a wooden bear who walked on all fours, turning his head from side to side, was made by August to stand up after ten steps, turn around, and walk on all fours in the other direction. But August knew that he would never make any real progress until he constructed the figures himself. Night after night, alone in his room, he practiced anew his old passion for woodcarving, angry that he had not known what his life was going to be, that no one had ever told him.

The clockwork toys, however clever internally, were externally crude in comparison with the carved figures and above all the dolls for which the town of Mühlenberg was well known, and August began to visit the toy shops and the doll-makers' shops with an appraising eye. Dolls at this period were enjoying a burst of popularity, and the Mühlenberg doll-makers were not behindhand in the realistic elaboration which was the order of the day. The older dolls with wooden heads, whose hair was painted directly onto the wood, had for a generation been replaced by china-headed dolls, whose hair was of flax, or of mohair, or even of real human hair. But the china heads were themselves giving way to elegant Parisian heads of tinted bisque, with luminous glass eyes. Even the bisque heads were rivaled in lifelike effect by wax heads, which in England were being made with real eyebrows, real eyelashes, and real hair, each hair being carefully inserted in the wax by means of a hot needle. Meanwhile the doll dressmakers of Paris had been startling the world with their exquisitely detailed costumes. German dollmakers could not ignore the latest foreign methods, and August listened attentively to the dollmakers' talk, taking from it what he needed. He began to purchase arms, legs, and hands from Johannes Molner, an old dollmaker who took an interest in the serious youth. The old man sometimes invited August to stay after the shop closed, and lighting up his meerschaum he would listen with amusement as the boy argued that ball joints should be added to the fingers of dolls, that the movable neck was still in a primitive state and might easily be improved, that movable eyes were only a first step toward total facial mobility. Herr Molner had a strong sense of proper limits, and no understanding of clockwork, but the boy's fire warmed him and he taught August what he knew about the art of dollmaking. He showed August how the porcelain head was hollowed out on top and bottom; inside, the eyes were fastened with wax and plaster to the two holes in the face. A wig of mohair was carefully glued to the top of the head. The body, of white kid, was lined with linen; between the linen and the kid, the edge of the porcelain bust was held in place.

The arms were attached next, fastened by iron wire fitting into iron hooks, and last of all the legs. August, curious about the substances of doll bodies, was instructed in the properties of kid, of gutta-percha, of papier-mâché dipped in wax. One day August brought Herr Molner a small gutta-percha hand, attached to an arm; the fingers were jointed, and a clockwork mechanism caused each finger to lift and lower in turn, after which the hand formed itself into a fist and slowly unclenched. Herr Molner stared for a long time at the little clockwork hand, and raising his troubled eyes declared that the proper end of a work of art was to arouse in the beholder a state of quiet reflection and not of astonishment, that the laudable realism of the nineteenth century, when carried too far, became a form of indiscretion, and that the hand in itself was extremely clever but not commercially practical. August, who had hoped for advice concerning the thumb, at first could not understand what Herr Molner was talking about; at the end he lowered his eyes, embarrassed for the kindly old dollmaker.

That spring, August gave his father a gift. Joseph removed the top of the shoebox, unwrapped the loosely folded brown paper, and discovered a mannequin not much longer than his hand. The plump little fellow was impeccably dressed in the manner of a fashionable burgher, in a tailcoat and vest; he had sidewhiskers and bushy eyebrows and wore a pair of bifocals low on his nose. A gold watch-chain hung in a graceful festoon from vest-pocket to vest-button. Joseph nodded his head slowly in admiration, and August strove to conceal his excitement as his father placed the little man on a table. A small lever was hidden beneath one sleeve. Joseph touched the lever and quickly removed his hand. The little burgher took three steps forward, and stopped. He reached into his vest-pocket and removed his watch. He brought the watch close to his face, raised his bushy eyebrows, and returned the watch to his vest-pocket. He took six steps forward, and stopped. He reached into his vest-pocket and removed his watch. He brought the watch close to his face, raised his bushy eyebrows, lifted his other hand and slapped himself on the forehead. Shaking his head, he replaced his watch. He took three steps forward, and repeated the first set of motions. He took six steps forward, and repeated the second set of motions. It lasted three minutes.

Joseph Eschenburg was delighted with the little man, whose miniature watch kept precise time, and he showed his pleasure in a way that moved August deeply: he replaced the mainspring with a much stronger one, and set up the little man in the window of his shop. There the clockwork burgher marched back and forth for a full sixteen minutes, taking out his watch and raising his eyebrows in surprise, while passersby stopped to look and point. The clockwork burgher brought forth smiles and laughter, and for a while business picked up noticeably. This gave August a wonderful idea: he would make automatons for his father's shopwindow. In this way he could justify his obsession while indulging it to the utmost.

The burgher was soon seen in the company of a little clockwork Frau in a feathered hat, who carried under one arm a Swiss clock from which, every five steps, a cuckoo suddenly emerged—whereupon the lady's mouth opened, her eyebrows lifted, her eyes rolled around. The clockwork burgher and the clockwork Frau, walking back and forth in states of continual alarm, proved highly amusing to all who passed by, and August began to add other figures in rapid succession: a little black schnauzer who ran alongside the Frau, stopping to bark silently each time the cuckoo leaped out; a young man of fashion who sat down on a bench under a linden tree, lazily took out his watch, and suddenly sprang up and hurried away, after which he returned to the bench and repeated the same motions; an old man bent over so that his dirty white beard trailed on the ground, as he carried on his back an elegantly reproduced grandfather clock. Already people spoke admiringly of the sixteen-year-old boy's shrewd business sense, a form of praise that pleased old Joseph but made August secretly uneasy. He felt that the business part of things was a mysterious and amusing accident that had nothing to do with clockwork at all, that some dangerous mistake had been made, that someday he would be exposed as a dreamer, a ne'er-do-well, a seedy magician in a drab green tent.

One day about a year later a well-dressed gentleman came into the shop, carrying an ebony walking stick whose ivory top was shaped like the head of a roaring lion. After a cursory examination of an ormolu clock, which he praised without interest, the man removed a business card and handed it to Joseph Eschenburg. Herr Preisendanz was the owner of one of the big department stores that were springing up everywhere in the new Germany, and he offered to purchase three of the clockwork figures for a startling sum. When Joseph replied that they were not for sale, Herr Preisendanz smiled, tripled the sum, and offered to purchase the entire stock of figures at comparable prices, even though not all were suitable for his purposes. When Joseph explained that his son had made them, and that they were not for sale, Herr Preisendanz narrowed his eyes, considered doubling the last sum named, but after a rapid examination of the old man's face—Herr Preisendanz had had dealings with these small-town shop owners before, some of them could be extremely stubborn— he decided to try another tack instead. He stated that he wished to bring Joseph Eschenburg's son back with him to Berlin, where he would be extremely well paid to make automated displays for the block-long shopwindow of the Preisendanz Emporium. He well understood that the prospect of parting would be a jolt to the old man, but he declared himself certain that the father would not stand in his son's way. Moreover, he would personally see to it that the young man was comfortably lodged.

Joseph listened gravely to all that was said and then called in his son. August was amused by the coarse-featured, red-faced man in his elegant clothes, not least because he so strikingly resembled a recent clockwork figure that had proved quite popular. But the offer frightened him; again he felt that somehow he was deceiving people, that they ought to realize . . . he wasn't sure what. Besides, he didn't in the least care for Herr Preisendanz and wanted to remain forever with his father, who understood him as no one else ever could. And Berlin was Prussia, he detested the very idea of Prussia. Without hesitation he turned down the offer, and was startled when his father said that every question had many sides. With grave graciousness the old watchmaker asked Herr Preisendanz to return the next day for a final decision. Herr Preisendanz, who had business to attend to, bowed slightly and took his leave.

Joseph Eschenburg knew perfectly well that the stranger from Berlin did not have his son's true interests at heart, and that the glib words about not standing in August's way had been uttered merely to win his compliance. But he was far too intelligent not to see that the offer was a very good one. The rich store-owner had mentioned a salary far greater than August could ever hope to earn in the watchmaker's shop, despite the recent increase in business; and Mühlenberg, though noted for its dolls, and even for its silverware factory, had little to offer in comparison with the Prussian capital. August ought to be given his chance; if things worked out badly, the boy could always come home. That very spring he would conclude his Gymnasium courses; a university was out of the question, for August showed little interest in formal study and had proved a restless and mediocre student. He seemed to look forward to nothing except working in the watchmaker's shop by day and constructing clockwork figures by night. And August had a gift, there was no denying it. The boy ought to be given his chance. It might never come again.

August Eschenburg

And so that summer, shortly after his eighteenth birthday, and rather against his own inclination, August Eschenburg parted from his father and traveled by coach and rail to the capital of the new Reich. Later he could recall nothing of this journey, and Berlin itself remained oddly shadowy in his memory, as if his attention had been elsewhere—although his memory of a particular stretch of shady side-street was so precise that he could still see the brilliant green reflection of heart-shaped linden leaves in a certain plate-glass window as well as in the individual dark winebottles behind the glass. It was along this street that he walked each day on his way from his two comfortable rooms on the fourth floor of a quiet boarding house to the hot, bright avenue where the Preisendanz Emporium was situated between a fashionable tobacconist's and a jewelry shop. August could no more tell you the name of that avenue than he could tell you how many Frenchmen had surrendered at Sedan, but he still saw clearly every gleaming item in the tobacconist's window, from the long, ebon-stemmed and silver-lidded meerschaum displayed in a case lined with blue velvet, as if the pipe were a violin, to the little bronze tobacco-grinder shaped like a shepherdess. The Emporium, which extended from the tobacconist's on one corner to the jeweler's on the other, was furnished with four large plate-glass windows in which were displayed, respectively: six female dummies wearing the latest Parisian fashions; a group of glittering optical instruments such as telescopes, ivory-handled magnifying glasses, binoculars, stereoscopes, and cameras; a handsome array of toys, from varnished rocking horses to onyx chess sets; and a nice set of mahogany bedsteads, mattresses, and elegant sheets and spreads. It was August's job to create miniature clockwork figures for three of these windows. For the fourth, Preisendanz had borrowed a splendid idea from one of the big New York department stores: on two mattresses displayed side by side, a wax figure and a live actor, both wearing striped pajamas, lay as if asleep, and spectators were invited to guess which was the real man.

August had to admit to himself that he found his new work unexpectedly pleasant. Much to his surprise he took an instant liking to the Preisendanz Emporium, whose insistent and even strident modernity was supposed to be a sign of the new Germany but revealed delightful contradictions. Thus the new plate-glass windows were inserted in a façade modeled on a Renaissance palazzo, and the new steam-powered elevators imported from America, which floated you up through all five floors, detracted not at all from the grand stairway of the ground floor, with its marble pillars and its air of old-world elegance. August saw at once that all these effects had been carefully planned by Preisendanz to attract a public easily stirred by two contradictory impulses: love of a vague, mythical, heroic past, and love of a vague, thrilling future representing something entirely new. Both loves betrayed a secret hatred of the present which August felt was the unspoken truth of the new order. But quite aside from these stimulating reflections he enjoyed the look and feel of the place: the thick rugs, the elevator boys in their red uniforms, the glass display cases that reminded him of a museum, the ground-floor drinking fountain that was said to be the first of its kind in Germany. The goods themselves were of high quality; Preisendanz, for all his vulgarity, had surprisingly good taste. But above all August enjoyed his work. He was given a workroom all to himself, on the fifth floor, and was supplied promptly with whatever he required. Never had his clockwork needs been so lavishly, so painstakingly, satisfied; it seemed as if his thought could instantly be turned into matter before his eyes. Preisendanz proved to be a keen and intelligent judge of clockwork figures, and was himself surprised at August's lack of historical knowledge of his craft;

August did not even seem to know that the great age of automatons was past, that it was already a quaint art-form whose true place was in museums and in the cabinets of private collectors, although it continued a last, desperate, and degraded life in fair booths and traveling museums. Preisendanz had been in London when the great Robert-Houdin had arrived from Paris with his Soirées Fantastiques and had displayed his famous pastry-maker, who emerged from his shop bearing whatever confections the audience had called for. It was all extremely clever, but Preisendanz had been somewhat disappointed; the automaton lacked the elegance of the best late-eighteenth-century examples. It could in no way compare, for instance, with the miniature automatons of John Joseph Merlin, a Belgian mechanist who had displayed his figures in London in the sixties of the last century, and whose fifteen-inch clockwork women were said to have imitated human motions with unusual precision, including motions of the neck, the fingers, and even the eyelids. He had seen one of these remarkable figures, badly damaged, in the collection of a viscount. Preisendanz had followed closely the vogue of life-sized automatons, for he felt those old mainstays of the exhibitions had unheralded commercial possibilities; and he himself owned a life-sized automaton writer, clearly based on the famous Jacquet-Droz figure, though no longer in working condition. To all this, August listened with a curious mixture of keen interest and indifference.

Preisendanz was pleased with August's first creation, a six-inch boy in short pants who played in turn with five exquisitely rendered miniature toys, the gigantic originals of which were displayed nearby: a Hampelmann or jumping jack, a little pull-along poodle on red wheels, a jack-in-the-box woodcutter with a little axe over his shoulder, a shiny rocking horse that was actually a rocking zebra, and a little easel on which with a piece of charcoal the clockwork boy drew, very neatly and clearly, a smiling clown.

At first August enjoyed the walk to and from his rooms

on the leafy side-street, with its delightful collection of shops: a shop with great wheels of cheese in every shade of orange and yellow, a bakery that sold thick black pumpernickel hot from the oven, a private doorway above a high brick stairway, a window displaying a collection of riding crops and shiny leather boots, a shop where gleaming pearly fish with glassy eyes and gaping mouths lay beside slices of brilliant yellow lemon, two private doorways above flights of stone steps, a window displaying a fine collection of hearing trumpets and wooden legs and glass eyes, a window with dark bottles of wine showing bright green linden leaves, and the corner to-bacconist's. His boarding house stood between the cheese shop and a glover's. But more and more he found himself lingering in the workshop on the fifth floor of the Emporium, and when Preisendanz gave him permission to remain over-night, and even supplied him with a Preisendanz mattress, August moved in permanently, though without giving up his unoccupied rooms on the side-street. He never quite under-stood why he wanted those rooms, which he never visited; perhaps they represented a possibility of independence from the Emporium, an independence which he liked to have at his command even though he never made use of it. Preisen-danz locked the Emporium every night at six, and was not displeased to have a light burning late on the fifth floor to discourage burglars. During the afternoon August would buy bread and cheese and fruit, which he brought to the work-shop, and sometimes at night, during a difficult stretch of work, he would leave the workshop and wander through the dark rooms of the department store with their rows of mys-terious and night-enchanted merchandise, lit by gleams from the gaslights outside.

Sometimes August was disturbed by the strangeness of his new life, as if it were all a dream from which he must wake up at any moment, but these very thoughts only made him throw himself more ardently into his work. Besides, he was engaged in an exciting new project.

One day Preisendanz had had the damaged, life-sized automaton writer delivered to the workshop, and August had carefully taken it apart in an effort to penetrate the secret of its construction. The external figure, a boy with curly locks, was stiff and crude in comparison with the delicate clockwork miniatures that August was constructing, but the internal clockwork was far more complex than any he had yet encountered. The boy sat before a small desk and held in one hand a quill pen. Before him on the desk was a piece of writing paper, and at the edge of the desk sat a small inkwell. Preisendanz, who had seen one like it in Paris, explained that the automaton was supposed to dip his pen into the inkstand, shake off a few drops of ink, and slowly and carefully copy onto the sheet of paper the words already written there. The automaton had left the proper spaces between words and, at the end of each word requiring it, had gone back to dot the i's and cross the t's. He could remember no other details. The piece of paper on the desk before the automaton boy bore the message, in English: "In the second century of the Christian era, the Empire of Rome comprehended the fairest part of the earth, and the most civilized portion of mankind."

August, while constructing miniatures for Preisendanz, labored over the life-sized boy writer for six months before discovering its secret: someone had removed three different sets of wheels, evidently with the intention of preventing anyone else from operating the automaton. After much experimentation August filled in the gaps, and called in Preisendanz to see the demonstration. Preisendanz was delighted, and wondered aloud whether they should start producing life-sized automatons. August, looking up in surprise, was shocked at this revelation of vulgarity. And once again he had the sensation that everything was uncertain, that things were bound to end badly.

He had learned a great deal from his reconstruction of the boy writer, especially about the internal structure of the hand, and at once applied his knowledge in a set of new miniature figures that surpassed all his others in grace and complexity. He improved the boy at the easel, who instead of drawing a simple clown now wrote in neat German script: "Ladies and gentlemen, welcome to the Priesendanz Emporium," after which he stepped back, examined his message, stepped forward, crossed out the "ie" and wrote "ei" above it, turned around, and bowed. At this point spectators on the sidewalk often burst into applause. August next improved his two other displays. For the window of optical instruments he had originally created a little man with binoculars around his neck, who strolled about, lifting his miniature binoculars to his eyes and examining various items about him, and finally turning to the spectators themselves. He had proved quite a popular little figure. August now added a second figure, who sat at a desk and made four different sketches of objects on display: a telescope on a tripod, a microscope, a stereoscope with a handle, and the miniature man with the binoculars. The little draftsman looked up from time to time at the object he was sketching, and bent over his work with a frown of concentration—never had anyone seen a figure so lifelike. For the window of life-sized mannequins he had originally created two fashionable clockwork women strolling along from dummy to dummy, glancing up and exchanging droll looks. He now added a miniature couturier, who at the bidding of the women took up a pair of little scissors, cut material from a bolt of cloth, and proceeded to make before their eyes a dress worn by one of the life-sized figures. The boy writer, the draftsman, and the couturier drew so many spectators that lines had to be formed before each window, and people were urged to walk slowly past and give others a chance to see. Business increased markedly, word began to spread; and all over the city people were heard to speak of the Priesendanz automatons.

It was inevitable that other large department stores should imitate the new Priesendanz attraction, and long before August had solved the mystery of the automaton writer, small moving figures had begun to appear in rival windows. Preisendanz followed these developments carefully, taking August with him whenever a new display appeared, but the rival figures were so awkward and elementary that they posed no real danger and indeed enhanced the reputation of the Preisendanz windows. Preisendanz feared, however, that the spread of his idea in even a crude and mediocre form would harm him by weakening the sense of novelty by which he had captured public attention, and in order to keep that sense alive he believed it was important to add new figures as often as possible. More than once he suggested to August that the production of new figures might be speeded up by certain simplifications, and more than once they had come close to quarreling, for August knew that his figures were still far too crude and was shocked at the suggestion that he ignore the direction in which his art was moving: the precise imitation of all human motions. Preisendanz had always backed down from an outright quarrel, for he was worried about losing the valuable service of his increasingly temperamental automatist, and in any case he as yet had no real rivals in the realm of window automatons. The three new figures had captured wider crowds than ever before, and he only hoped that August would complete his next figures while he had the public in the palm of his hand. But then a development took place that changed everything.

An older department store, four stories high, had for a long time stood on the same avenue, one block over and on the other side of the street. Indeed, Preisendanz had chosen the location for his Emporium partly with the idea of taking over the first store's business, and this he had largely succeeded in doing. The older store held a clearance sale, the building was sold, and for a time the plate-glass windows stood empty, except for a forgotten tape measure in a pile of wood shavings. But then the new owners arrived, and changes began taking place. The display space was enlarged, the old plate glass was replaced with new and larger sheets of glass, hydraulic elevators were installed, an elaborate doorway with an awning sprang up, boxes of new merchandise began to arrive—and the opening day of the new store, called Die Brüder Grimm, was fast approaching. Preisendanz had been annoyed by the catchy new name, with its shameless appeal to the German hearth, and was surprised to learn that the new owners were in fact called Heinrich and Johann Grimm. The brothers came from Hamburg, were brisk young men in their twenties who both wore their hair *en brosse,* and appeared to know exactly what they were doing. All this was disturbing enough, but the blow came on opening day: the gleaming new windows were unveiled to reveal artful displays of first-rate merchandise, which served as background to a remarkable set of automatons.

Preisendanz saw at once that the eight-inch figures could not compare with his in complexity of performance, fluidity of motion, and precision of detail. Their fingers moved only at one joint, their movements were stiff and inelegant, they performed the most elementary motions. And yet they possessed a striking and unmistakable quality, one might say an originality, that lifted them far above other automatons of their degree of complexity, and challenged even his own. For these new figures were somehow—and it was difficult to find the precise word—somehow sensual. They were by no means openly and shamelessly erotic, for the respectable crowds on the fashionable avenue would have been shocked and disgusted by too direct an appeal to their animal natures, but the skill of these automatons, one was tempted to say their brilliance, lay precisely in the degree to which they were able to appear decorous while conveying an unmistakable flavor of lasciviousness. In the window of women's fashions, for example, two female automatons strolled up and down before the spectators and did not even look at the clothes on display. One was a woman and one a girl of perhaps sixteen. Both had bright blue eyes and blond braids. They were dressed impeccably in the latest French fashion, and yet their anatomy had been distorted slightly to produce a definite effect: their rumps had been exaggerated in a manner approaching that of certain picture postcards, and had been given a faint but distinct motion under the closely clinging fabric of their boudoir gowns, and their breasts were of a kind rarely or perhaps never seen in natural females, suggesting rather the protuberant dream-roundness of adolescent fantasy. The Frau and Mädchen seemed thrust out before and behind, and brilliantly approached indecency without stepping over the line of the respectable. At each end of their walk, they sat down on a couch and crossed their legs, revealing for a moment a fetching glimpse of tight silken stockings—a glimpse, moreover, that changed slightly each time. Even the window of toys was a triumph of lubricity: in a circus ring a little horse went round and round—the movements were awkward and elementary, though the horse was painted a lovely shiny black—and on top of him stood a bareback rider with her arms spread and one leg lifted behind her. She was half the size of the other automatons, as if to express her toylike nature, and she was capable of so few motions that in reality she was little more than a doll. But she had been dressed in flesh-colored tights, an allusion no doubt to the famous English bareback rider, and although one could not quite accuse the toy of impropriety, still her legs and little buttocks had been carefully molded to be as suggestive as possible, an effect heightened by the black-mustached ringmaster in his shiny leather boots who from time to time gave a rather awkward crack with his whip. Preisendanz could not swear to it, but each time the horse carried the bareback rider around a certain turn he had the fleeting sense that he could see a disturbing darkness between her legs.

These effects he meticulously pointed out to August later that morning, but August's contempt for the workmanship was insurmountable. Preisendanz urged him to ignore the workmanship for the sake of the effects, but August replied that the ludicrous effects were a result of the inept craft, and that personally he saw nothing desirable about a fat behind. The automatons, although worthless as clockwork, did in his opinion betray one technical skill: the flesh had been rendered remarkably well, so well that one might almost call the result brilliant, though it seemed a shame such talent should be wasted on trash. Preisendanz saw at once that it was so: the flesh of those women was terribly desirable. Once again he tried to impress upon his stubborn automatist the hidden virtues of the rival automatons, but August, who at first had laughed gaily, became abruptly sullen.

Preisendanz knew that the world of modern commerce obeyed one all-embracing principle: novelty. This principle was divisible into two laws: novelty is necessary, and novelty never lasts. The second law might also be phrased: today's novelty is tomorrow's ennui. The Grimm brothers had introduced a novelty, and had thus dealt the Preisendanz Emporium a blow, but it remained to be seen how quickly the public grew tired of those sensual toys. An opening-day crowd was deceptive, for people were of course curious and out for bargains. Preisendanz was prepared to be patient, before approaching young Eschenburg again.

By the end of the second week the crowd of window-shoppers before Die Brüder Grimm had nearly doubled, and with a shock Preisendanz saw why: all the automatons had been replaced by new ones, in the same sensual style. The audience was therefore provided with the same piquant effects, yet at the same time given the stimulating sense of something entirely new. One of the new figures, in a daring climax, lifted her dress all the way to mid-thigh in order to display her peacock-blue Parisian stockings. Preisendanz hurried back to his Emporium and in the workroom on the fifth floor asked August how soon his next figure would be ready. August wasn't certain: two months, perhaps three . . . he was working on a new motion. To August's amazement, Preisendanz suddenly lost his temper, but at once regained it. Pacing up and down with one hand held behind his back and one hand lifted in emphatic gesture, he explained to August that he could no longer afford to wait so long; the volume of business for the past week had already fallen off, though not too sharply, but it was a sign of worse to come unless the crowds were drawn in. August's automatons, as automatons, were of course far superior to the Grimm automatons, but as crowd-drawing devices they frankly left a great deal to be desired. People wanted to see automatons of the risqué variety, and they wanted to see as many as possible, and for that they were willing to do without a perfection of craft which in itself was admirable but which perhaps smacked too much of a bygone age. August replied that if Preisendanz was correct, then the people did not want to see automatons at all but simply plump behinds and fat thighs, in which case—but here Preisendanz begged leave to point out that motion was part of the piquant effect. He was certain that August could capture it and indeed, with his greater mastery of motion, surpass it readily. August was about to reply that surely there was a contradiction somewhere, since Preisendanz had just been urging him to do away with craft, when suddenly he lost interest and fell into gloomy silence.

When Preisendanz left, August knew that something serious had happened, and that his pleasant way of life was being dangerously threatened, but he felt certain that Preisendanz would come round to the correct view of things when he saw August's newest automaton. If he reduced his sleep to four hours a night, and worked with supreme concentration, perhaps the new figure could be completed in as short a time as one month. He had already lavished untold hours upon her, and she promised to be his finest creation. She was a young woman, a year or two younger than August, and even he realized that he was half in love with her. He felt like another Pygmalion, but a Pygmalion who knew the secret of bringing his statue to life. He had labored lovingly over the neck and face until she far surpassed his earlier figures in her capacity to reproduce human motions and emotions: her nostrils could dilate, and even her lips possessed an admirable mobility that greatly enhanced her range of expressiveness. She was constructed to walk across the window space and try on a fur coat that a comical, pot-bellied salesman would hold out for her; she would then look at herself in a three-way mirror, experience indecision, and at last, in a burst of joy, decide to purchase it. After paying the correct amount in beautifully reproduced little bills and coins, she would walk along in her new fur coat, crossing the entire display area until she disappeared behind a curtain. The little drama called for a high degree of facial expressiveness, and August was still dissatisfied with the mirror episode, which did not quite reveal her inner struggle. But far more important was the final walk, when every motion of her body must express her delight. There was no doubt: he had fallen in love with her, and felt that he was giving her the glorious gift of life.

Business declined slightly during the next week. Preisendanz was anxious, but not yet alarmed: there was still no sharp falling off, and he felt he could afford to wait until August was ready with the new figure, about which the boy had been unusually secretive. Meanwhile Preisendanz fired the sleeping actor, removed the wax figure, and placed in the window of beds and mattresses a pretty twelve-year-old girl, the blue-eyed daughter of a woman friend who was a painter's model. The girl wore a short, frilly nightdress and was instructed to make the beds with different kinds of sheets, plump up the pillows, flop about on the mattresses, and in general keep moving about as much as possible. Preisendanz had selected her with great care: she had an angelic face and no breasts, so that she could appear in his window without scandal, but her legs were coming along nicely, and the movements of her little rump were really very appealing.

A week later there appeared in the mattress window of Die Brüder Grimm two new automatons. They were blue-eyed girls in frilly nightdresses, and the way they wriggled about was simply—well, indecent. The crowds enjoyed it immensely, for it seemed to be a great joke—a joke unmistakably directed at the Preisendanz Emporium. Preisendanz was frantic, and was only partially soothed when August, looking pale and drawn, assured him that the new figure would be ready by the end of the week. Preisendanz wondered whether in the meantime he might try a new idea: the girl in the nightdress might be placed in a tub of water, from which she could emerge shivering to take refuge in a warm, soft Preisendanz bed. The wet nightdress clinging to her ripening curves might be extremely effective. He was still turning this idea over in his mind when August announced that his figure was ready. That night, behind the closed curtain of the display window, Preisendanz watched the young woman walk across the floor, try on her fur coat, and walk back, while August stood by, pale and grim. As August watched the shy maiden he forgot his exhaustion, for he knew without arrogance that he had created a work of supreme beauty. When it was over he turned to Preisendanz, who appeared strangely meditative. Preisendanz muttered a few words, praised the wrong thing (the putting on of the coat was in fact a little awkward, the shoulders needed a bit more work), and left for dinner. August, elated by his triumph, and puzzled by Preisendanz' curious behavior, returned his studio to work on the shoulder: the left one in particular was unsatisfactory. When he opened his eyes he realized he had fallen asleep at his workbench. Before him lay his Fräulein, a few hands, an envelope. There was still a half hour until opening time. He washed quickly and hurried down to the display window, where parting the back curtain he stopped in amazement.

There in the window, before a small crowd only some of whose eyes lifted to the parted curtain where he stood, two hideous automatons were marching back and forth. Their gestures were jerky; they had plump calves, fat behinds, and grotesquely protuberant bosoms. Their eyes rolled, their shiny red mouths appeared to smirk. He recognized them at once as the work of his crude rival. Wind from a concealed bellows was being blown at them through a tube, so that their dresses were pressed against their bodies and sometimes fluttered up.

August, feeling dazed, hurried away to find Preisendanz. He found the owner in the toy window, over which the front curtain had been drawn. Preisendanz was pacing back and forth excitedly while a handsome young man with thick, wavy yellow hair was setting up a pair of ugly child-automatons, one of whom was dressed in nothing but a pair of white drawers with pink bows. Preisendanz, who kept looking at his watch, seemed irritated at seeing August, and, while keeping his attention upon the child-automatons, asked whether August had not received the note which had been sent up to him. August, who suddenly realized what was happening, became strangely calm and returned to his workshop, where opening the envelope he read that financial considerations of the most urgent kind had regrettably forced Herr Preisendanz to terminate their association. A generous sum of money was enclosed. August removed a single small bill—enough to cover the cost of the train and coach home—gathered his few belongings and his Fräulein, and was about to leave when he noticed the life-sized boy writer in a corner. Stepping over to it, he prepared to remove the three gear trains he had added, thought better of it, left the room, and took the first train back to Mühlenberg.

THE MAGIC THEATER

August had not seen his father for nearly two years. Their meeting was tearful, as their parting had not been, and once again August took up his work in the watchmaker's shop. Joseph seemed remarkably unchanged, as if time did indeed obey different laws in the shop of clocks, but August sensed a slight difference that at first he could not account for. He soon realized what it was: his father moved a little more slowly. It was as if Joseph's body had aged while his face had remained unchanged by time. For that matter, August had seen in his father's face how he himself had changed, and his reflection in that mirror startled him and made him seem strange to himself, even though he knew perfectly well that he had grown at least a foot over the last two years and now sported a thick, soft mustache. But the change that most troubled him was in the repairing of watches. Although he enjoyed his old trade, and worked for his father as a virtual partner, he found himself impatient at the loss of hours from his true work. Preisendanz had spoiled him—he had forgotten what it meant not to labor day and night on the increasingly complex and beautiful processes of automaton clockwork—and he had to struggle against an inner restlessness that seemed to him almost a betrayal of his love for his father. Joseph knew where his son's heart lay, and urged him to reduce the hours he spent in the shop, but the very fact of his secret restlessness made August unwilling to accede to it. Meanwhile he had his nights, and his precious Sundays. He converted his old room into a workshop, and with the money he had saved as well as the money he now earned he ordered materials from Paris, London, and Berlin. During his Berlin years he had become slowly adept in the highly complex matter of ordering supplies, and although he could never hope to duplicate the superb conditions of his work-life in the Emporium, when the need for a tool, or a rare kind of cloth, or a chemical dye was quickly satisfied by the expert knowledge of Preisendanz, and although he now had far less money at his command, nevertheless he was soon able to work well enough under the new conditions. And he was free of Preisendanz. He no longer had to care about store windows, and customers, and the imitation of clothes and goods, but could devote his energy to the only thing that mattered: the creation of living motion by the art of clockwork. Never again would he permit his creatures to be used in windows, never again would he sell them into slavery. The crude old automatons in his father's window were permitted to remain, for he thought of them as toys, but he never added a new one.

One morning about two years after his return to Mühlenberg, a stranger walked into the shop. He was a handsome, slender young man of about August's age, dressed in a beautifully tailored dark-blue suit which he wore with a careless ease and which, August noticed with amusement, precisely matched the color of his eyes. He held under one arm an elegant walking stick with a top shaped like the head of a grimacing troll—it was really a clever piece of work, and August for some reason imagined it coming to life and biting a finger—and he carried in one hand a parcel wrapped in brown paper. He asked in a Berlin accent if he might speak to August Eschenburg. August was alone in the shop that morning and at once presented himself to the elegant stranger, who proceeded to study him with a cool, amused frankness that might have been insolent had it not seemed so good-natured. A dim memory stirred, but August could not quite place him. "I've a package for you," the stranger then said, and handed him the parcel, adding the single word: "Hausenstein." August, amused and not at all irritated by the deliberate air of mystery, opened the package. It contained his miniature boy writer. He looked up in surprise, and recognized the blond-haired youth whom he had fleetingly seen in the window with Preisendanz.

"I thought you might want it as a keepsake. A pleasant little souvenir of the dear old days. Ah, the days of our fled youth—pity they didn't flee a little quicker. It's quite clever, Eschenburg—brilliant, as a matter of fact. They're forgotten now—the fools are more fickle than even I supposed. You're still at it, I trust?" He glanced around keenly. "Incidentally, I'm the fellow whose trash drove you out. Do you have a few minutes? Odd question to put in a clockshop."

Preisendanz had hired him out from under the noses of the Grimm brothers, who within a year had sold their premises to an insurance agency and returned to Hamburg. Hausenstein—he never gave his first name, and August never asked—had been paid a small fortune to supply his new master with an uninterrupted stream of automatons cleverly combining the genteel and the lascivious, and although for a time he had found the work stimulating, it had soon begun to pall. He could not look forward with excessive ardor to spending the rest of his life in the production of rubbish for the likes of Preisendanz and the beloved German *populus*. Oh, he knew it was rubbish, and he was superb at his job precisely because he knew exactly what was required—and now that he had a bit of money he wanted to strike out on his own. He had recognized at once the astonishing quality of the Eschenburg automatons, for he himself possessed a small talent in that line, and he had recognized at the same time that those automatons were fated to be driven out by the sort of cheap approximation that was the true symbol of the new age. Since this fate was inevitable, he had decided to be its instrument. It amused him to calculate to the finest hair's-breadth the precise level of vulgarity to which one must sink in order to gain the hearts of the modern masses—the German masses in particular. But really the entire century was rushing toward a mediocrity that a youthful cynic could only find delightful, justifying as it did his low opinion of mankind in its present form. Nietzsche, bless his romantic soul, had invented the Übermensch, but Hausenstein had countered with a far better word: the Untermensch. By Untermensch he certainly did not wish to suggest the rabble—they were far too poor and hungry to concern themselves with anything at all except scraping out a miserable living in a wretched world. No, the Untermensch was a strictly spiritual term, and by it he meant the kind of soul that, in the presence of anything great, or noble, or beautiful, or original, instinctively longed to pull it down and reduce it to a common level. The Untermensch did this always in the name of some resounding principle: patriotism, for example, or the spirit of mankind, or social progress, or morality, or truth. The Untermensch had always existed in the world, but until the second half of the nineteenth century he had remained a relatively modest force, only occasionally rising up to tear down something he could not understand—a statue, say, or a book, or a liberator. But in the present half-century the spirit of the Untermensch had spread until it had taken over the Western world—it ruled in America, in France, in Britain, and above all in that newest nation, that quintessentially modern nation which had patched itself together in the latter days of history, Germany herself, the immortal Vaterland. In Germany the spirit was far more pervasive than elsewhere, and far more dangerous, for there the mediocre and modern joined hands with darker and more ancient forces; the union was perfectly expressed in the Prussian army, which combined the modern idea of efficiency with ancient bloodlust. But he was digressing; he meant only to suggest that he was a student of the modern age, and as a student he had seen clearly that the automatons of Eschenburg must give way before the automatons of Hausenstein, that cheerful apostle of the Untermensch.

Well, it had been amusing for a time, and he had made quite a pile; but even he had to confess that a prolonged submersion in the rank swamplands of the modern mass soul was not the most pleasant way in which to spend one's bit of time on the merry way to extinction. Besides, it was clear that even the most tedious cynic such as himself could not be a cynic except in relation to an ideal, and it therefore followed that even he, and perhaps he especially, had a sense of what was being dragged down. His dabbling in the clockwork line had enabled him to recognize that August's figures were brilliant, and entirely out of place in the windows of the Preisendanz Emporium. He, Hausenstein, confessed to a weakness for brilliance, on the rare occasions when he came across the real thing; and his wealth now permitted him to indulge a whim. In short, he was proposing to finance August Eschenburg in the little matter of an automaton theater. He had the place selected already, in Berlin; he himself would manage the theater but would exercise no control whatever over August. He did not pretend to be disinterested: he had reason to believe that he would rake in a nice profit, and in addition he was curious to see the direction Eschenburg's talent would take, once left to its own devices.

August listened to all this with amusement, with interest, and with growing irritation. He felt irritated because he felt tempted; somehow or other, this debonair and embittered visitor had given voice to one of his deepest longings. Even during the Preisendanz years, when from the sidewalk he had watched his early automatons going through their motions, the idea of a theater had scattered its seeds across his mind; and since his return to Mühlenberg, the idea had taken secret root and begun to grow. And now, at the touch of Hausenstein's words, it had burst into dangerous flower. August could not make sense of Hausenstein: he distrusted him, and yet there was a disarming frankness about him that left August puzzled and uneasy. Why had he come? Hausenstein was obviously bored, bored deep in his spirit, in the manner of someone whose intelligence is far greater than his talent; but ennui had distractions far more amusing than the automatons of a watchmaker in Mühlenberg. Was he—this mocker of men and self-declared apostle of the Untermensch—was he perhaps secretly afraid that he too was one of the mediocre? Did he need to bathe himself in the fluid of another's creativity, in the hope that he would be washed clean of all that was common in him?

August, uncertain, asked Hausenstein to return in the evening and visit him in his workshop. That evening he showed Hausenstein the figures he had created in the last two years, and only when the demonstration was over did he realize that he had been testing Hausenstein: one false note of praise, one inaccuracy of judgment or coarseness of perception, and August would have sent him off with his tedious boredom and his mocking mouth. But Hausenstein, no less than Preisendanz before him, knew what he was talking about. Without becoming falsely earnest, without altering his manner of worldliness, amusement, and contempt, Hausenstein spoke with authority and precision about what he called the Eschenburg automatons. He said he liked women with more blood in them, and told August to visit brothels for the sake of his art; he pointed out a very minor flaw in one figure that only an expert could possibly have detected. His praise was also precise; and he compared the Eschenburg figures in detail with the greatest automatons of the last hundred and fifty years. Technically, August had carried the art beyond any point it had reached before; and it was clear that he would never rest until he had created a figure capable of all the motions of the human musculature. In this striving, there was madness; but no doubt it was as good a way as another to pass the time.

Hausenstein spoke a great deal that night, and not only about the art of automatons. Not all of what he said made sense to August, for Hausenstein, despite his gift of exact criticism, was given to the spinning of elaborate theories, but one idea did make a strong impression on him. Hausenstein maintained that the nineteenth century was above all the century of motion. By this he did not mean simply, or even primarily, that the age was obsessed with speed: frankly, trains bored him, though this did not prevent him from seeing their spiritual significance, and incidentally there was a rather nice description of a moving landscape watched from a train in a little poem by Verlaine in *La Bonne Chanson* which was probably the first description in French verse of this very modern phenomenon. Someday he would perhaps write a little paper comparing such descriptions with earlier ones of landscapes glimpsed from coaches. But trains were only a crude expression of the century's love of motion, which was far more strikingly expressed in its arts and entertainments. The new painters in France, for instance, might speak as much as they liked about sunlight and chromatic values; what struck an observer above all in the curious products of *l'impressionisme* was the sense of leaves stirring, of reflections rippling, of air trembling—it was an art consisting entirely of shimmer and vibration, of solid things broken into trembling points: sunlight as motion, the universe as nothing but motion. But such effects were capable of only a moderate development and would inevitably be replaced by the far more compelling illusions of motion that the century was already developing in its popular entertainments. Photography, that characteristic invention of the age, was considered by many learned gentlemen to have driven painting into the excesses of the modern school, but these same gentlemen would do better to realize that *l'impressionisme* was merely one expression of a much wider tendency. More than a decade before Daguerre displayed his first light-picture in 1839, a far more important discovery had been made in the realm of optics. It was discovered that an image cast onto the retina remains there for a fraction of a second after the object is removed. This profoundly significant phenomenon—surely August had heard of persistence of vision?—had been demonstrated by means of an ingenious toy. It was called the thaumatrope, and was no more than a small paper disk with a different image on each side: a bald man on one side and a toupee on the other, a parrot on one side and a cage on the other. Strings were attached to the opposite ends of the disk to permit twirling. When the disk whirled about, the two different images merged into one: the bald man wore his toupee, the parrot sat in the cage. But the thaumatrope, while demonstrating the principle of persistence of vision, did not present the illusion of motion. It was in 1832 that Monsieur Plateau invented his phenakistoscope, lovely name, that slotted disk attached to a handle and spun before a mirror. On one side of the disk a number of drawings were arranged in phase, and when the disk was rotated before the mirror, the reflected image viewed through the whirling slots became a single continuous motion: the little girl skipped rope. Thus was born the moving image, which already in this crude and childish form surpassed the effects of the clockwork pictures of the previous century. There had followed a stream of charming and ingenious toys, each improving the illusion of motion and each bearing a splendid name—but he would not bore August to death with descriptions of the zoetrope, the praxinoscope, and other such toys of genius. He would mention only that as early as mid-century the magic lantern had been combined with one of these devices to project moving images on a screen. And at this very moment, in Paris, the brilliant Emile Reynaud, using his own praxinoscope, was projecting colored moving pictures onto a background cast by a second projector. These pictures were all of course painted by hand, but it was only a matter of time before the photograph itself—that authoritative illusion—would be used in place of the hand-painted picture. Indeed, serial photographs had already been invented across the ocean, in dear old America; it remained only for some sublime tinkerer to discover a practical way to produce and project them. Then a new art would be born, and the century's striving for the illusion of motion would at last be satisfied. It was amusing that Daguerre, the inventor of light-pictures, had also invented that hoary popular entertainment the Diorama, which had drawn large crowds early in the century with its quite different illusions of motion, produced by ingenious lighting effects, and doomed to extinction. *L'impressionisme,* the Diorama, pictures that move— these were the inventions that he found far more revealing than the railroad and the dynamo, for in these arts the century's love of motion had invaded a medium that by its very nature was motionless.

And that brought him round to August; he apologized if he had talked too much already, he hated bores. For August too was part of the century's great tendency. True, he had chosen an eighteenth-century form, one might say an obsolete form, but he had developed it so much further than the old automatists had done that in his hands it became almost new.

He had simply carried their experiments to an extreme—and what more modern than this lack of a sense of bounds, this need to take something as far as it would go? The art of the automaton was a dead art—he hoped August did not deceive himself into thinking otherwise—but in August's hands it had taken on a last, brilliant life, it had achieved a realism surpassing the old art of waxwork, for his fanatically imitative figures seemed to live and breathe. And because the age desired the illusion of motion, and because the devices that made pictures move were still in a crude state, and because the photograph had not yet been adapted to its final purpose—because of all this, the time was right for an automaton theater. He did not want August to think that he hadn't considered the matter rather carefully.

August scarcely knew what to make of this speech, which he had not been able to follow in all its turnings—he himself was accustomed to thinking mostly with his fingers—but one thing struck him forcibly: he did not like to be told that he was out of step with his time, or in step with his time. He felt that his work had nothing whatever to do with such questions, which obscurely threatened him by ignoring everything that mattered most. What mattered was that one day in a drab green tent something had lit up in him and had never gone out. The art of clockwork was his fate, but clockwork was also a sort of accident; what he cared about was something else, which had no name and had only an accidental relation to time and place. He did not say any of this to Hausenstein, but he was grateful to Hausenstein for having made him have those thoughts. The long speech had another curious effect: somehow, and he could not quite say why, he felt sorry for Hausenstein, and knew that he must never reveal this to him. The evening exhausted August, but before it was over he had decided to go to Berlin. He would need six months in Mühlenberg to solve three clockwork problems. Hausenstein said that he himself planned to knock about for a few months before getting down to business. When he rose to leave, he drew on his gloves, picked up his walking stick, and remarked, "Amusing, isn't it?" Suddenly the grimacing troll snapped its jaws shut. August was uncertain whether Hausenstein's words had referred to the clever troll, to the automaton theater, or to life itself.

A few weeks later August received a postcard from Genoa, which Hausenstein said was hot and boring, and three days after that a postcard from Vienna, containing the single word "Ciao," and then nothing at all for five and a half months, when he received a card from Berlin, telling him what train to take and where to get off. Somewhat to August's surprise, Hausenstein was there at the station to meet him, looking entirely the same, and behaving as if they had last spoken a few hours ago. It was ten at night and August had been traveling since early morning. Hausenstein hailed a cabriolet and soon August found himself clattering through a district of narrow streets and bright-flaring gas jets that lit with a smoky green-yellow glow the masklike faces of Damen and Herren on the sidewalks. There were shouts of laughter, a light piano tune burst from a passing doorway, through a dimly lit window came a clash of steins. A lady in a great wide-brimmed hat and a feather boa walked arm in arm with a little pale bald man who had a large, beautiful, shiny-black mustache. The cab turned into a darker but still lively side-street and stopped. August hoped the hotel room would not be facing the street. Hausenstein, carrying one of August's traveling bags, led him to a narrow doorway half-illuminated by a nearby light. He drew out a great iron key, opened the door, and lighting a match led August along a narrow, dark corridor at the end of which was a curtain. August followed him through the curtain; the match went out. Hausenstein fumbled about in the blackness and at last lit a gaslamp. August saw that he was standing at the back of a high small room with rows of seats and a stage. "Like it?" said Hausenstein, and still for another second or two August could not understand where he was.

Hausenstein had chosen a location at the edge of the café and theater district, and after a week or two at a nearby hotel August simply moved into his theater, sleeping on a cot in the small room behind the stage. It was not so much a theater as a small hall that, before Hausenstein had rented it for August's use, had seen a wide variety of arts and talents: a lecture on the science of phrenology, an exhibition of anatomical waxworks, a showing of *images animées,* a demonstration of the wonders of electricity, a stereoscopic slide show devoted to modern Egypt, a concert on the Mechanical Orchestra, an evening of songs and recitations by a troupe of child actors, and a program of nature-whistling in which Professor Ekelund of Uppsala imitated the calls of more than two hundred birds and beasts. Hausenstein, reciting this history gleefully to August, compared the stage with its red curtain to a redheaded whore welcoming all comers. "You will be her aristocrat," he added, trying to make August smile, but August was engrossed in practical problems. The small theater had scarcely more than a hundred seats, but even so the stage was far too large for his purposes, and he set about constructing a small portable theater, about the height of a man, that could be placed in the center of the stage and illuminated from within. The structure of the little plays or pieces proved far more difficult, and here Hausenstein revealed himself to be full of helpful and technically expert advice. At the same time, Hausenstein was overseeing a host of matters down to the smallest detail: the painting and restructuring of the hall, the design of scenery for the portable theater, the advertisements. The new name of the theater was to be painted on a red awning hung over the door, but he decided not to make the name public until three weeks before opening day. Meanwhile, August labored day and night over the construction of automaton actors. The performance would consist of three pieces, each about fifteen minutes long, with two interludes upon which he worked no less fiercely.

Four weeks before opening day, yellow handbills began to

appear on streetlamps and in shopwindows, announcing in handsome black-letter the opening date of what was called the Automaton Theater. Advertisements were placed in the leading newspapers. One week later, a red awning was unfurled over the doorway, bearing the words: Das Zaubertheater.

Hausenstein had not doubted for a moment that he could fill the small theater on opening night; the test was whether it could be filled night after night. The first show was therefore of vital importance. August had worked down to the last minute, making infinitesimal changes that suddenly became a matter of life and death; he continually rearranged the 121 seats, sitting in each one and worrying whether the view was good. Tickets were sold out in advance; Hausenstein wished to admit standees, but August refused so vehemently that there was no arguing with him. And so, on opening night, the people came and took their seats, it was really quite simple. August had planned to sit in the audience, in the back row, but suddenly he abandoned his seat and spent the performance restlessly pacing the room backstage. As a result there was a single empty seat on opening night. Hausenstein made a brief introductory speech in front of the closed, large curtain, then stepped into one of the wings, where he remained throughout the entire performance.

The curtain opened to reveal August's theater, itself provided with a curtain, as well as with an elaborately carved proscenium arch flanked by fluted Corinthian columns. The automaton theater was illuminated from the large stage by gaslights which went out as the curtain slowly opened upon a moonlit scene in a forest glade. It was Hausenstein who had persuaded August to begin with *Pierrot,* the piece that of the three permitted the most striking scenic effects and that, because of its association with the pantomime, was best suited to accustoming the crowd to automaton silence. This was the romantic Pierrot of recent imagination, the artist-lover hiding behind his comic mask, but in August's handling of the pale, white-gowned figure with his long sleeves and his row of big buttons, who with blood-red roses and a lute pursues without success his charming Columbine, the melancholy and despair of the spurned lover slowly deepened and darkened until, in the final scene, it seemed to become entwined with the moonlight itself, and under the brilliant, dissolving power of the mysterious moon was transformed into a frantic gaiety: the piece ended in a wild and silent dance, in which Pierrot with his dark eyes and broken lute seemed to soar above his despair and to dissolve in the beauty of the moonlit night. The piece lasted twelve minutes and forty seconds. Hausenstein, watching from the wings, saw that the audience was held.

The first interlude followed immediately. The curtain of the automaton theater opened to reveal a little grand piano, held in a spotlight. From one wing a little man in black evening dress strode forward. At the piano bench he threw out his tails, sat down, and played three of Schumann's *Kinderscenen*. The audience, who had remained respectfully silent after *Pierrot*, burst into applause after each piece, most vigorously after *Träumerei*. At the end the little pianist stood up and bowed gracefully. Someone called "Encore!" and the cry was taken up, but the stern little pianist strode off the stage. Hausenstein saw that an encore would have brought down the house.

The second piece, which lasted fourteen minutes, was heavily applauded: it was entitled *Undine,* an adaptation by August of the story of the water sprite and the knight, based on the novella by Fouqué. Hausenstein had been concerned lest this well-worn darling of the romantic age should prove an embarrassment, but the enchanted landscape was extremely effective, and the Undine automaton had an expressivity of gesture that was unsurpassed. The second interlude was a pas de deux from *Swan Lake,* danced to piano accompaniment; Hausenstein wondered whether the reappearance of the pianist—actually a second pianist exactly resembling the first—was not a mistake. But he was far more concerned about the success of the third piece, which August had created himself. Entitled *Fantasiestück*, though bearing no relation to Schumann, it opened with a display of toys in a toy-store window. The audience was looking at the display from the inside, for the plate glass was toward the back of the little stage, and behind it passed several recognizable Berlin types, who stopped to look before passing on. Slowly it grew dark—Hausenstein noted that the lighting effects were simply splendid—and in the dim light of the gas jets the dolls began to wake. Slowly they rose, waking to fuller and fuller life but never losing a certain clumsy, jerky motion, until with a burst of energy they joined hands and danced round and round, the wooden soldier and the English duchess and the engineer on the Nürnberg train and Madame de Pompadour—and as the first light of dawn began to break, their motions grew heavier and heavier until at last, yawning jerkily, they resumed their rigid positions in the light of another morning. The curtain closed. August, lying on his cot and smoking a French cigarette, heard dim applause. All at once the door opened and Hausenstein was seizing him by the arm and drawing him out onto the stage. Hausenstein led the applause; the audience rose to its feet. August, looking with alarm at all the standing people, kept brushing cigarette ash from his sleeve, and suddenly left the stage in confusion.

It had been a superb success; the question was whether it would hold. Hausenstein was disappointed when the next morning only a single review appeared, and not in a major paper. The review, which asked whether such a production, for all its ingenuity, could properly be called artistic in the truest sense, was nevertheless favorable, and Hausenstein trusted that other notices would follow in due course. Indeed, the very next day a brilliant review appeared, taking issue with the first, and expounding the principles of automaton art with clarity and precision. The long article was signed *Ingeniosus*. "Now there's a fellow who knows what he's talking about," said Hausenstein, who had circled several paragraphs admiringly, and who in fact had written the review himself; but other reviewers soon took up the cause. Meanwhile the 121 seats of the Zaubertheater continued to be filled night after night, and August worked on another piece with which to vary the program; eventually Hausenstein hoped to have a different set of pieces every week. Together they made innumerable minor improvements in lighting and scenery, and one day toward the end of the fourth week, when cries of "Encore!" followed the performance of the *Kinderscenen*, the little pianist returned to his bench and brought down the house with a Chopin mazurka. While still working feverishly on his larger piece, August substituted for the pas de deux, which had never quite satisfied him, a passionate violinist with long black hair, who along with the surprisingly well-liked pianist gave a spirited performance of the first movement of the Kreutzer Sonata. One day a long review appeared, not written by Hausenstein, wherein August Eschenburg was called a master. The house continued to fill each night, and Hausenstein noted with satisfaction that some of the faces were the same.

Within three months two rival automaton theaters opened. Hausenstein had anticipated and indeed hoped for this development, since not only did it show that automatons had taken hold of the public imagination, but also it provided the critics with a chance to compare the masterful figures of the Zaubertheater with the blundering mechanisms that had sprung up in its shadow. More disturbing to him was the notable increase in other forms of automaton art. Some showman had constructed two life-sized automatons based on the old Jacquet-Droz figures, and his exhibitions were drawing large crowds; another exhibitor opened a hall of waxworks whose grisly effects were enhanced by clockwork mechanisms that caused arms to lift, eyes to move back and forth, and heads to turn. These rather tedious effects, insofar as they were a sign of automaton fever, were all to the good, but nevertheless they threatened to detract from the Zaubertheater by

making clockwork gestures overly familiar and therefore unmysterious. A certain nostalgia seemed to be taking hold;
imitations of eighteenth-century toys began to appear in expensive shops, a puppet theater opened, and a professor of
philology at Heidelberg took time out from his scrupulous
investigations of Sanskrit to write a thoroughly idiotic article
in which he defended Maelzel's chess-player against the
American denigrator Edgar Allen [sic] Poe, despite the fact
that Poe had practically stolen his account from Sir David
Brewster's *Letters on Natural Magic*. The famous, fraudulent
chess-playing automaton, invented not by Maelzel as the mis-
informed professor supposed, but by Wolfgang von Kempelen, had long ago been destroyed by fire, an event which the
professor suggested had been contrived by enemies of the
Second Reich. It was all the most pitiful patriotic trash, and
was yet another sign of the startling interest in early automatons, an interest that Hausenstein feared for a second reason
as well: those in sympathy with new forms of art might be led
to associate Eschenburg with outmoded forms. And it happened: an article in a radical journal of the arts contained a
paragraph attacking the Zaubertheater as a force for conser-
vatism against which all lovers of artistic freedom must fight
to the death. The blundering writer was under the impression
that Eschenburg was an exhibitor of chess-playing automatons, and the journal was reputed to be read only by its con-
tributors, but still it was a sign. Yet Hausenstein's disturbance
over the increase of rival forms of automaton art, and his fear
that the Zaubertheater might be misunderstood in certain
influential quarters, were slight in comparison with a more
general uneasiness: he feared automaton fever itself. An ap-
parent sign of triumph, such sudden and intense ardor, such
flaming interest, could not conceal from him the terrible fate
of all bright flames. And well he knew the restlessness, the
secret boredom, of the last quarter of the nineteenth century,
which sometimes seemed to be rushing headlong toward some
unimaginable doom.

And indeed, before another six months had passed, automaton fever seemed to be dying out. Exhibitors of life-sized automatons could no longer fill their halls, which now were devoted to spirit-rapping and demonstrations of the wonders of chemical science. One of the rival theaters had already closed and reopened as a cabaret, and the other had begun to alternate evenings of the automaton theater with evenings devoted to much-improved magic-lantern shows and scientific lectures. Attendance at the Zaubertheater was still good but had fallen off after the first triumphant months; some evenings only half the seats were filled, although weekend performances continued to draw full houses. August had created a small group of fanatically devoted admirers, but the circle had not widened; there were so many other distractions, so many other entertainments. By the end of the first year August had created nine different pieces, which he presented in varying combinations of three, but it was becoming clear that attendance had fallen off sharply: some nights, only a handful of the faithful were present. It was about this time that a new theater sprang up, and threatened the very life of the Zaubertheater.

Hausenstein had repeatedly urged August to enliven his repertoire in certain ways. He had suggested that Undine's girlish breasts, concealed by her long hair, be teasingly exposed, significantly enlarged, and piquantly provided with stylish French nipples pointing slightly upward. He had also suggested that Columbine, whose charming buttocks might well be plumper, should fall down during her dance and, throwing up her handsome legs—real works of genius, those legs—expose herself briefly to good effect. And he had urged replacing the rather stodgy interludes with lighter entertainments—for instance, a cabaret singer kicking her legs. But to all such suggestions August opposed a contemptuous silence. His later pieces had moments of dark, disturbing beauty to which Hausenstein was by no means insensitive, yet even as he experienced them he could not help wondering whether the audience was quite up to it. August was more and more clearly using automaton art to express spiritual states, and such lofty experiments were bound to seem rather confusing to all but the most stubborn adherents of the Zaubertheater. And now, four blocks away, the new theater had appeared.

It was called Zum Schwarzen Stiefel—At the Sign of the Black Boot—and August first learned of it through Hausenstein, who insisted on bringing him there one night. From an iron post above the door hung a long, tight-laced, shiny black boot, from which emerged a pink calf, a pink knee, and part of a pink thigh, all seen through the meshes of a black net stocking. The lifelike leg had been executed in three dimensions, and was illuminated by two lanterns, one red and one green. Inside, in a narrow corridor, August's eyes smarted with cigar-smoke. A tight-corseted woman with half-bared, very round breasts, between which sprouted an artificial rose, took their tickets. The rose disturbed August; he wondered whether it had artificial thorns. The theater itself was somewhat larger than the Zaubertheater—Hausenstein estimated a seating capacity of 180—and not only were all the seats filled but people stood along the walls, waving at their perspiring faces with gloves or magazines. Most of the audience were men, but a number of well-dressed women were also present. The curtain of the large stage opened to reveal a smaller theater, obviously modeled on August's automaton theater, but nearly twice the size. As the curtain lifted, a rollicking cabaret tune was struck up on a real piano at the side of the large stage; the music continued during the entire performance. There were three pieces, without interlude. In the first piece, six cabaret dancers, about a foot high, came strutting onto the stage. They wore long, full skirts beneath which one glimpsed petticoats and frilly drawers; their glossy black boots were laced very tight, and their large breasts were partly exposed. They kicked their plump legs high, strutted about with a great rolling of rumps, and sat down from time to time with parted knees. Though the clockwork was elementary, care and attention had been lavished on their black silk stockings, their petticoats, their drawers, above all on their wriggling buttocks and bouncy breasts. At the end, each buxom Mäd-chen placed her hands on the plump shoulders of the girl before her and they all tripped off prettily with a great shak-ing of skirts. In the second piece the same six girls returned, and performed precisely the same motions, but this time they wore only glossy black boots, black silk stockings encircled above the knee by brilliant red garters adorned with black rosettes, and loose-clinging drawers trimmed with ruffles and ribbons and reaching scarcely to mid-thigh. The illusion of naked, trembling flesh was aided by the reddish light that dimly illuminated the bodies and to some extent concealed gross errors of construction. Their big breasts were impossi-bly round and firm, and their nipples bright rosy red, but their elaborately clad buttocks were parodic masterpieces of round, rolling plumpness. Though lacking skirts, the autom-aton maidens reached down as if to lift them slightly for their kicks—a clumsiness that seemed only to delight the audience, who applauded lustily as the six smiling lasses wriggled into the wings. August left in the middle of the third piece. The curtain lifted on a drably lit stage showing a crooked fence across a moonlit field. From one wing entered an automaton lady dressed charmingly for a country outing. On her head was a wide-brimmed straw hat heaped with grapes and cher-ries, and she wore a peasant dress with long full skirts and a trimmed white bodice with short puffed sleeves and a square neckline prettily revealing the tops of her breasts. She wore glossy black boots and long white gloves. Walking somewhat clumsily to the fence, she leaned her elbows on the top rail with her back to the audience and looked out across the moonlit field. There now entered from the other wing a male automaton wearing a black top hat and a handsome cutaway coat and matching trousers and carrying a gold-handled cane. When he came up to the girl, who did not seem to notice him, he stood gazing at her without expression. Reaching forward

with his cane, he slowly lifted her full skirt and flouncy petticoats to reveal a charming pair of legs in black silk stockings,
encircled above the knee by bright red garters adorned with
black rosettes. The girl, paying not the slightest attention to
him, continued to gaze out over the moonlit field. Rather
clumsily the male automaton continued to lift her garments
until he had exposed two very round and pink and plump
buttocks nicely set off by the glistening black of the stockings.
When the skirt and petticoats lay over the back and head of
the girl, the man proceeded to undo his trousers—he touched
a lever in his side to release his belt—and stood sideways for
a few moments contemplating his long red erection which
resembled a bloody limb. Turning to the girl, he appeared to
be having some trouble as August rose and left. On the street
Hausenstein spoke of a certain *je ne sais quoi* of aesthetic mastery which distinguished one artist's work from another, of
the unknown artist's sure and penetrating grasp of the national soul. August was not amused. "These same burghers
demand first-rate lenses for their cameras and they'd be en-
raged if they received a cheap substitute—yet when it comes
to clockwork they can admire the cheapest, most technically
mediocre work. So long as it's accompanied by lots of fat
behinds."

"It's what I've been saying, my friend: your good blue-
eyed German likes plenty of beef on his plate and plenty of
beef on his women. It's good middle-class training from first
to last: Podsnappery, as the English Raabe calls it. The heavier
the better, in art as in gravy. You won't listen to me—well,
listen to the applause at the Black Boot. You've got to throw
the dogs a little meat, and while they're licking their chops
you'll have time enough to go to work on their souls—though
frankly the blessed German soul is much overrated in these
latter days of her most glorious century and reminds me of
nothing so much as Maelzel's or rather Kempelen's chess-
player: a hollow sham with a humbug inside. Did you know,
by the way, that Maelzel also constructed an ear trumpet for

Beethoven? Yes, there you have the German soul in all its dialectical splendor: the maestro listening to the universe through the ear trumpet of a successful fraud. This same Maelzel, charming fellow, built a mechanical orchestra of forty-two life-sized musicians, which had quite a vogue at one time. He also swindled the public into believing that he'd invented the metronome—not bad for one lifetime. But to return to the admirable precision of German cameras: those estimable lenses you spoke of are responsible for some highly detailed and extremely instructive photographs which one can see in certain private collections. I think the real trouble with Germany is that she's too close to Paris: visions of *le beau monde* torment her dark, uneasy sleep. Of course *le beau monde* for your blue-eyed German means fashionable women in expensive underwear. Fifteen hundred years ago, Rome tormented her in the same way—your blue-eyed Visigoth must have dreamed of dark-eyed Roman ladies lying back in elegant tunics, eating grapes, and revealing from time to time a fetching glimpse of the latest in Latin under-tunics and leather breastbands. In any case, I merely wish to suggest that capitalism and history are both against you, if you persist in serving up visions of high beauty to an upright citizen of Kaiser Wilhelm's Reich. He won't stand for it for very long; give him his roast beef and French underwear."

August was less tolerant than usual of his friend's facile manner, which seemed to attack the very idea of seriousness while continually inviting a serious response. He returned to his theater workshop in a bad humor. He recognized no law requiring the world to pay the slightest attention to him or his work, but by the same token he saw no reason to bend himself out of spiritual shape in the hope of pleasing a corrupt public. He would do what he had to do, in obedience to the only law he knew, and if they did not like it—well, so much the worse for him, and perhaps for them too. His ambition was to insert his dreams into the world, and if they were the wrong dreams, then he would dream them in solitude. August now threw himself feverishly into a single long piece that, even as he worked on it, he knew would surpass his finest achievements in automaton art. The eyes and especially the lips of his creatures were capable of a new expressivity so subtle and striking that his automatons seemed indeed to live and think and suffer and breathe. But while they represented yet another advance in the direction of precise imitation, another stage in the mastery of realism, at the same time they seemed to reach a height far above the merely material, as if realism itself were being pressed into the service of a higher law. So, at least, Hausenstein expressed it, when the new composition was completed, although he added with a weary sigh that he supposed it would lose them half of the remaining faithful. And yet, one never knew; the dark-eyed suffering automaton girl, whom August called simply Marie, had a brilliancy of flesh, a radiance, that was quite remarkable, and in her walk there was a new suggestion of ripeness, of sexual wakening, of sensual knowledge too innocent to be entirely conscious of itself yet disturbedly aware of the dark secret of menstruation: it was a sense of girlhood blossoming into womanhood, a sense of womanhood about to wake from the long sleep of girlhood and needing only the kiss of the prince to make life stir in the sleep-enchanted palace that was her heart. August, barely listening to Hausenstein, knew that he had created her with tenderness, with something akin to love-anguish, and he stood before his creature now as if in awe of his own work. "Yes yes," he said, when Hausenstein was done, "but you see—she's alive."

Hausenstein proved correct: Marie captivated her audience, but only after that audience had dwindled to twenty or thirty a night. At such a rate the Zaubertheater could not long survive, and August noticed that Hausenstein spent less and less time in the largely empty theater, as if avoiding an unhappiness. He no longer urged August to appeal to a wider public, but seemed content to let him go his own way—a change that would have pleased August had it not so clearly been the result of giving up. And far, far back in his mind there was something that disturbed August, something he could not quite bring to awareness. At times he felt that it was all very familiar, that his life was repeating a pattern whose outcome he did not quite want to remember.

One night when the performance was over and the audience of fifteen had slowly begun to put on their coats, August, who had silently come out to take a seat and watch the last few minutes, heard a young woman say to another woman: "It's remarkable, but I think I could watch her night after night and never have enough. But I wonder how they manage. The man who runs this place is a martyr." "Oh, but you know what they say," her friend replied. "It seems this Hausenstein has a finger in more than one pie. I've heard he runs the Black Boot—and, my dear, I can assure you it is not a *maison de souliers.*"

August had a sensation that the wind had just been knocked out of him. At the same time, his heart was beating violently, blood was rushing through him. The figures were not the same, but he knew there had been something familiar about them: the extremely well-rendered flesh. Feeling a little dizzy, and with a strange tremor in his stomach, he set off in search of Hausenstein. The ticket woman at the Black Boot, who remembered August, seemed to evade his eyes; no, she hadn't seen Herr Hausenstein recently. August was relieved to see that the artificial rose had been replaced by a bunch of real violets, rather drooped and faded in the warm, oppressive air. He bought a ticket and entered the smoky hall. Every seat was taken, people stood against the walls. Nothing had changed: the six automaton girls in their boots and stockings lumbered about the red-lit stage. Pushing his way past people standing in the aisle, who strained around him to see, August made his way to a little stairway at the left of the stage that led through a curtain to the door of a dressing room. The door was locked, but when he rapped it was opened quickly by a thin, flour-pale man in suspenders and shirt sleeves who was holding by the ankle a naked leg in a black boot. "I'm looking for Hausenstein," said August, who saw that the room was empty. "Who the devil are you?" said the man, but August had already left. Perhaps he was crazy, after all it was only a rumor. . . . Out on the street he breathed deep, wiped the back of his hand slowly across his closed eyes, then set off for the Zaubertheater. He had not even locked the outer door: it could have been vandalized. In the dark empty theater, lit only by dim gas jets, he stumbled over the leg of a chair. "So there you are," said Hausenstein, emerging from a wing onto the stage. "I've been trying to get hold of you. Rather careless of you to leave the—" "You make them," said August, and sat down exhausted in the front row. Up on the stage Hausenstein appeared to freeze; August had the impression that he would move off jerkily, with a faint whirring sound. But Hausenstein was a far more convincing figure: his motions were superbly smooth, though with a telltale sense of brilliant contrivance. "I was wondering how long it would take you to congratulate me," he remarked, stepping forward and sitting down on the edge of the stage so that his legs dangled a few feet before and above August. "Besides, I don't precisely make them: I oversee. But you should have recognized my work—I'd know yours anywhere."

"Why did you do it?" His own voice sounded weary to him; he must sleep.

"Sheer love of the art, of course, and then there's the little matter of"—he rubbed two fingers briskly against the thumb—"filthy lucre. Our Zaubertheater has fallen on evil days. When you refused to do homage to the noble buttock"— he shrugged. "After all, I know them better than you do. But don't look so downcast. The proceeds are what keep you afloat."

"Not any more. I'm through."

"I was afraid you might take it badly. That's why, when you failed to recognize my work—and I did bring you there myself, pray remember—I hesitated to insist. Listen, don't be a fool. Tainted money, eh? A bit too literary: Pip and Mag-witch. Where else will you get a chance like this? I have news for you, my gifted but oh so innocent friend: automatons are dead. A handful care—they're not enough. Oh, who knows, perhaps if we held on for twenty years, for thirty years . . . even so, you are about to become outmoded. *L'image animée* is the wave of the future: I've explained it to you before. My friend, you are a brilliant poet writing a late-nineteenth-century poem in Middle High German: three scholars, one with a hearing difficulty, one with an unfortunate *tic douloureux,* and one requiring a bedpan, compose your audience."

"I express what I have to in a particular medium. What else is art? I don't study fads and trends."

"But I do, and I tell you, my friend: the day of the automaton is over."

"As I conceive it, the day has never even begun. But this is a useless discussion."

"And therefore quite artistic, at least according to one of the century's more charming notions—though I'm afraid the boyfriend of Beatrice might have disagreed. Who cares where the money comes from? Turn the sow's purse into a silk ear."

"It's not that, exactly. You should have told me. You're playing some kind of game. . . ."

"I'm a playful fellow—it's my artistic nature. Look, I know them: they're swine. I supply them with troughs. It amuses me; many things do. I like to see them prating about Liebe and Schönheit—and coming to the trough in the end. Did you notice, my inattentive friend, how many of the faces are familiar? They start out at the Zaubertheater and end up at the Schwarzen Stiefel: yes, it pleases me to make certain experiments, I won't deny it. Let me tell you something. When I was a lad of sixteen I went about with a blue-eyed maiden from a cultured family. Or to be more precise: the father was the owner of a pork butcher shop and the mother read Kleist and Nietzsche and Baudelaire and played Liszt and Wagner on the pianoforte. She took an interest in me, lent me books, and was in every way so superior to her empty-headed daughter that I soon dropped every pretense of caring about the girl and looked forward only to my next dose of spiritual food from the lips of the mother. I wasn't by any means unaware of the more material charms of my maternal Beatrice, but I no more thought of violating that shrine than I thought of attempting to discuss the Übermensch with her daughter. Need I say more? One twilit afternoon, as I turned the pages of a Chopin nocturne while she played, she seemed to grow faint as she neared the end of the piece, and as the last chords died away I was astonished to feel her head against my shoulder. Like a nice young idiot I asked her if she wanted a glass of water. She asked me to lead her to the couch. She was very direct. One detail I remember quite vividly: at the moment all youth dreams of—I had never been with a woman before, and had to be shown how to make her wet—but at that famous moment I saw, not far beyond her tense, flushed face, which appeared to be the strangely distorted mask of the woman whose soul I adored—I saw, lying upon a little mahogany table, a copy of volume two of *Dichtung und Wahrheit*, from which she had earlier read me a passage in order to compare it unfavorably to the nervous prose of Kleist. It was then I realized that art is nothing but a beautiful cool hand placed by a woman, sometimes not very carefully, over her hot pudendum. She spoke to me of beauty and the soul, but she really meant to speak of less rarefied matters. During her orgasms, which she herself compared to the Liebestod, she was fond of sighing out "Beautiful . . . oh, beautiful . . ."—a chant varied by the frequent interpolation of choice obscenities. Our meetings grew less and less artistic until one day— but that, my friend, is a story I shall save for my memoirs. I still have a dread of pork butchers. And so at the tender age of sixteen I learned an important secret: all words are masks, and the lovelier they are, the more they are meant to conceal. If it pleases me to be an unmasker—why, all to the good, I serve the fatherland in my own generous way. They chatter about the soul, I give them what they really want, and in the process I satisfy a sense of world-irony and a love of truth. Yes, I drag them down, the swine—I drag them down."

"But that makes you one of the Unter—"

"Yes?" said Hausenstein sharply, but August had caught himself, though not in time. The half-spoken word seemed to float in the space between them, preventing speech. Hausenstein slapped angrily at a fly on his sleeve. After a while he said, "Well. You'll stay?" August looked up in amazement.

"So you're going, eh? Splendid. And what will you do? Spend the rest of your life tightening springs in a clockshop? With me you could—oh, to hell with it. It's been an instructive evening, I always enjoy talking to a genuine artist, however passé."

August felt a burst of pity for Hausenstein, and hoped he would say no more.

"And let me tell you something, Eschenburg: you aren't that pure. You think you're the purest soul on earth, but you knew the theater was started with the money I made from Preisendanz. Who cares if it continues courtesy of the Black Boot?"

Wearily August answered, "I don't think I'm pure."

"Just too pure for me, is that it? Too pure to dirty your hands with my filthy money? And I'll tell you something else: you're not much of a friend. The minute something happens that doesn't suit your taste, it's good-bye friendship. I can't trust you. There's something cold about you. . . ." He stood up. "You just sit there. . . ." August looked up wearily and saw Hausenstein staring down at him with glowing bitter eyes. Had he hurt him that much? August felt bone-weary and he seemed to have a headache in the center of each eye. Hausenstein turned suddenly and walked with rapid sharp steps along the stage and down the wooden stairs at the side. He appeared to be leaving brusquely, but suddenly he sat down in the aisle seat, eight seats away from August.

"It's been a long night. You have a difficult temperament,

August. I too upon occasion have been known to be less than charming. Look, we've been together a long time. No one knows your work the way I do. No one." He paused. "You look tired. Get a good night's sleep. I'll see you in the morning." There was a pause, and he stood up violently. "Where will you ever find a friend like me?" Turning on his heel, he strode down the aisle. August heard his steps in the corridor and the sound of the outer door closing.

For a long while he sat there, trying to change his mind. He knew Hausenstein cared about him, and he asked himself whether he was being a bad friend. But he felt he could no longer trust Hausenstein. It was as if some boundary had been crossed, after which trust became impossible. Those naked automatons were a parody of everything he believed in. Hausenstein couldn't understand, because he believed in nothing. But that wasn't so: he believed in August. Or did he? Did he want him to fail? Did he take some secret delight in undermining the Zaubertheater? Did he want to drag him down into that trough of his, whose true vice was not its filthiness but its coziness, its air of conspiratorial chumminess, its secret banality masquerading as boldness? These were not the questions you asked of a man you called a friend. And yet, aside from Hausenstein, August had no friend. He was alone. August felt a deep pity for himself, for Hausenstein, for the Zaubertheater, for the universe. Suddenly he remembered that something was bothering him, something Hausenstein had said. What was it? Yes: that he would see him in the morning.

August left that night, taking with him half his creatures and leaving behind enough of them so that Hausenstein might continue operating the Zaubertheater if he wished. After all, it had been paid for with his money. August felt no desire for revenge, only a compelling need to be alone. He never saw Hausenstein again. At this point his recollections became brisk and fragmentary: he wandered with his creatures from town to town, renting small halls where he could, and staging performances in makeshift miniature theaters that were sometimes little more than a large empty box with a single hastily painted backdrop and a crude lamp that threw distorting shadows. The performances were sometimes well attended, but the audiences were generally scanty and a little confused. People seemed to come out of curiosity, as they might come to see a ventriloquist, a Fireproof Female, or a magician, and the Automaton Theater left them with a feeling of puzzlement, as if they had expected something else, something a little different. Hausenstein was right: automatons were dead. Here and there a face lit up with enchantment and understanding, and once a young woman burst into tears during a performance of *Pierrot,* but far more often there was coughing, a creaking of seats, a fanning of flushed cheeks. Once he heard someone say, "It must be some sort of trick— that box must have a false bottom." Tired, always tired, he moved from town to town; often he thought of the magician in the drab green tent. Yes, the art of the automaton was a magical art, for when all was said and done there was something mysterious and unaccountable about clockwork: you breathed into the nostrils of a creature of dust, and lo! it was alive. And so the art of clockwork was a high and noble art: the universe itself had been constructed by the greatest clockwork master of all, and remained obedient to mysterious laws of motion. And on the moving earth, all was ceaseless motion: wind and tide and fire. One day, coming to still another town, August read everywhere of preparations for a fair. And he was pleased: in the rented tent, not green but yellow-brown, he displayed his automatons before children.

He decided to return to Mühlenberg; perhaps he could take up his old trade. But first he wanted to pay a visit to Berlin. He arrived at night and went with wildly beating heart to the Zaubertheater, but the Zaubertheater was no longer there. A small, flourishing restaurant stood in its place, but so transformed in look that he had to stare very hard to be certain. The doorway had been widened and replaced with glass, a glass window had been built into the outer wall, the corridor wall had been torn down, and the stage itself had vanished into thin air. Only the old florid decorations high up on the ceiling remained to tell their tale. August was not unhappy. He would have liked to order a light dinner with a glass of wine—the hake looked first-rate—but the menu in the window was forbidding. A woman inside looked up at him with a frown; he stepped away from the glass. His coat was shabby, his hair long and unclean. On an impulse he decided to seek out the Black Boot, but that too was gone: in its place was a night club of a somewhat shady kind. Hausenstein was right: they were deader than a doornail. He thought of paying a visit to the Preisendanz Emporium but was suddenly afraid it might not be there; he wanted something to remain. He took the last train that night.

The train for Mühlenberg does not go as far as Mühlenberg itself, but stops at Ulmbach before continuing to the southwest. At Ulmbach August learned that the coach would leave in forty-six minutes. It was a sunny afternoon. Leaving his battered traveling bag at the coach house, but carrying his rope-tied suitcase of automatons, August took a walk to the back of the coach house and down to the small and nearly dry river, spanned by a wooden bridge. On the other side of the river was a small wood, beyond which he saw factory smokestacks. He crossed the bridge into the wood, spotted with sunlight. He looked for a shady place where he might sit down and eat the pear in his pocket. The wood was deserted; it appeared to be dying. He found a shady spot under a broad, decaying tree. He recognized it as a linden and thought, Hausenstein would have said something witty about that: Unter den Linden. He kicked away a mulch of old leaves covering its half-exposed roots. Sitting down wearily between two roots and half-closing his eyes, he felt shut away peacefully from the river and the factory. He noticed that his suitcase was half-sunk in the leaves and shifted it slightly. There were many leaves lying about, brown leaves and green leaves, and leaves that were green and brown together. August had a sudden idea. Laying the suitcase on its side, he began covering it with leaves. It was done quickly: the leaves had been lying in a depression, and the suitcase was well buried.

For it often happens that way: Fate blunders into a blind alley, and even an entire life can be a mistake. Perhaps one day a child, playing in the leaves, would discover a funny old suitcase. August leaned back against the linden and tried to understand. Was it really his fault that the world no longer cared about clockwork? He supposed it was: Hausenstein had explained it all to him a dozen times. But was beauty subject to fashion? He did not understand. What was a life? One day his father had opened the back of a watch and shown him the wheels inside. Was that his life? A bird inside a funny paper man, the boats in the picture that suddenly began to move, a perspiring magician in a drab green tent—were these the secret signs of a destiny, as intimate and precise as the watermark on a postage stamp? Or were they merely accidents, chosen by memory among the many accidents that constitute a life? He tried desperately to understand. Had it all been a mistake? His art was outmoded: the world had no need for him. And so it had all come to nothing. He had given his life away to a childish passion. And now it was over. He was terribly tired. Sitting under the warm shade of the linden, August grieved for his lost youth. Slowly his eyes closed, and his head fell forward.

August woke with a start. The sun shone brightly through the leaves of the wood. He had dreamed of his rooms in the boarding house near the Preisendanz Emporium. He took out his watch: he hadn't missed the coach. It was warm in the shade. A thrush landed on a branch of the linden, paused as if looking for something, and flew away. Suddenly August looked about in alarm. Where was his suitcase? Where? Stolen while he slept? Thieves in the wood? How? Where? He remembered.

He replaced the watch in his pocket and leaned back

against the linden. His heart was beating quickly, and he noticed that a hand was trembling. It was warm in the shade. Two factory smokestacks showed bright white through the trees. August felt that he needed to rest for a long time. But his little nap had refreshed him.

A short while later, he picked up his suitcase and started back to the coach house.

II

A Protest Against
the Sun

It was an absolutely perfect day. Her father at once objected
to the word, looking at her over the tops of his glasses and
nodding morosely in the direction of a loud red radio two
blankets away. Elizabeth laughed, but she knew exactly what
she meant. She meant the day was so clear that you could see
all the way across the Sound to a tiny cluster of three white
smokestacks on blue-green Long Island. She meant the far-
off barge, moving so slowly it was barely moving. It was the
rich dark color of semisweet chocolate. She meant the water,
dark blue and crinkled out there, smooth and greenish brown
between the sandbar and the beach. She meant that yellow
helicopter, flying high over the water toward the Sikorsky
plant. She meant that orange-and-white beach ball, that
grape-stained Popsicle stick, that brilliant-green Coke bottle
half-buried in the sand. A white straw was still in it. She meant
that precise smell: suntan lotion, hot sand, and seaweed. She
meant the loud red radio. She meant all of it.

"Still," she added, shading her eyes at the helicopter, "I
suppose it would be even more perfect with a blimp. Do you
remember that incredible blimp? Nanny from heaven? What
in the world ever happened to blimps? At least we still have
barges."

It was her mother who took it up. "Oh yes: Nanny from
heaven. I'll never forget the look on your face as long as I

live." Her own face glowed with it; drowsy in sunlight, Elizabeth smiled. She was just exactly in the mood to be drawn into the circle of family reminiscence. But it really had been incredible: mythical. It was a summer day in her childhood. They had been on this same beach. She remembered nothing except the blimp. There it suddenly was, filling all the sky like a friendly whale—like a great silver cigar—like nothing on earth. It was better than balloons, it was better than a walrus. She had looked up, everyone had looked up, because really there was nothing you could do when a blimp appeared except look up. They always frightened her a little but they were so terribly funny: strange and funny as their name, which of course was the wrong name as her father patiently explained. But still. And so the blimp appeared. And suddenly, it was so wonderful, the sky was full of falling things. Swiftly they came slanting down out of the sky, and all at once the little parachutes opened up, green ones and red ones and yellow ones and blue ones: and slowly slanting down they fell far out in the deep water, and then close by in the shallow water, and then on the sand. People shouted, jumped up to catch them, ran into the water. Elizabeth wanted one so badly that she felt she couldn't stand it; she wanted to cry, or die. But she stayed very still, she was in awe. And then one landed near her, the little colored cloth at the end of the strings came fluttering down, and she pounced. And it was hers. And it was bread. Two slices of white bread in a little package. And her father said, "Nanny from heaven." And so she said, "Nanny from heaven."

"Have you seriously failed to deduce the connection?" said Dr. Halstrom.

Elizabeth turned in amazement. "What in the world are you talking about?"

Her father raised his eyebrows in surprise. "You asked what happened to the blimps."

"Yes? You know what happened to them? What happened to them?"

"Did something happen to the blimps?" said Mrs. Halstrom.

"You noted the absence of blimps," said Dr. Halstrom, "and you noted the presence of barges. It occurred to me, in the best manner of contemporary thought, to draw the inevitable conclusion. Consider," he continued, lowering his voice and leaning toward Elizabeth, "the shape of barges. Carrying off the blimps: you can bet your bottom dollar."

"What?" said Mrs. Halstrom. "I couldn't hear you. Bess! What did he say? Tell me what's so funny! Did something happen to the blimps?" Then she too was laughing, because there was laughter; but they wouldn't tell her what he had said.

It was a lovely day. The sun burned down. Elizabeth pressed her back and shoulders into the army blanket. Sand was wonderful: it was soft and hard at the same time. It was such a good idea to come to the beach. With momentary irritation she recalled how the trip had very nearly failed to come off. She was suddenly furious. The day had been on the point of foundering because Dr. Halstrom had a paper to finish. She had fretted away the whole morning, exasperated by the unexpected change of plan. It was unfair. He sat shut up in his study on a Saturday in August. It was outrageous. She had set her heart on it. He had been sharp at breakfast, sharp and withdrawn. By noon she no longer cared. She said she no longer cared, but she was desolate. But then he emerged at ten of one, apologetic and triumphant. They had thrown things in the car and left. The tide was out, but that was nothing. They had the whole afternoon.

Elizabeth lay on her own blanket but she had carefully made the edge overlap the edge of her parents' blanket. She liked to lie down in the sun and they liked to sit on low beach chairs on their blanket while they read. The chairs were so low that her parents could stretch their legs straight out. But the books! It was absurd. Her mother had brought *Persuasion*. But she was afraid to get sand in it, because it was a present from Elizabeth, and so she had brought a library novel with a vase of red roses on the cover; she said it was awful. Her father had dragged along a fat seventeenth-century anthology, two collections of Milton criticism, and a library novel showing an airplane with a dagger going through it. She herself was no better: *Théâtre de Molière*, Volume II, and a paperback Larousse, really a ridiculous choice for the beach, and, because she had secretly known it was a ridiculous choice, a science-fiction thing called *Dune,* which Marcia had recommended, and which was even more ridiculous since she hated science fiction with a passion. But she liked Marcia. So she had brought *Dune.* It was all ridiculous. Her father had made a joke about carrying coals to Newcastle and *Dune* to the dunes. He had asked her how she was dune. I'm dune fine, she had said. Her three books lay in a neat pile near her straw beach bag and her father's books lay scattered on the other side of her. It was ridiculous; absurd. She was lying on a sunny blanket in the middle of a library. Her mother had read for a while and then put aside her awful book, taking off her white beach hat with the broad brim and throwing back her head. Her beautiful hair in sunlight was the color of mahogany: but soft. And finally she had folded up her chair and lain down in the sun. Dr. Halstrom had continued reading, but at last he too had put his book aside, and sat with half-closed eyes looking out at the water. Elizabeth thought he was a dear to have come. He looked almost boyish with his little carefully groomed blond beard so lightly streaked with gray that you could scarcely tell. He had the fine smooth skin of a man not much exposed to weather. His face and forearms had color but his broad chest and upper arms were pale.

"You'd better put your shirt on, Dad. You don't want to burn."

"Oh, no. Thanks, Bess. I'm all right. I never burn, except with moral indignation. Plato was right: in a properly ordered republic, that radio would not be tolerated. The lack of consideration of that woman."

"I can ask her to turn it down."

"Unfortunately I believe in her God-given right to torment me. I was thinking, though, that your book looks rather forlorn. It ought to be called *Forlorna Dune*."

"If you keep mocking my book I won't tell her to turn it dune."

And her father laughed, showing his boyish smile with the two handsome hollows in his cheeks like elongated dimples.

It was a lovely drowsy day. Elizabeth felt that her pleasure was probably excessive; her father said she shared with her mother a tendency toward the excessive. Even to Elizabeth the morning's anger and desolation seemed a little excessive. After all, she was no longer a child. It wasn't as if they couldn't have gone to the beach the next day, or even the next. But it was already late in August; she would soon be away at school again; somehow these little family outings had a way of being too casually proposed and too easily abandoned. If she hadn't fought for it, the day would have been lost. Lately, for no particular reason, Elizabeth had felt the absence of family occasions. Nothing whatever had changed at home: the treasured closeness was there. But she felt there was a carelessness, a danger, in just going on thoughtlessly from day to day. There were only a certain number of days in a lifetime, after all. She really didn't know how to express it, but she felt that just by existing, just by letting the days flow by, they were all threatened in some way: as if deterioration were bound to set in. She couldn't account for it. Maybe she was growing morbid. But there were times she felt like saying, as if she were old and they careless and young: don't you realize that nothing lasts? That one day it will be too late? She had no idea what it would be too late for; she barely knew what it all meant. But she did know there were times when she needed to assert her family feeling.

Dark thoughts for a sunny day: she hoped she wasn't growing morbid. It was so nice to lie all lazy in the sun. The blanket warmed by the sun made her think of pajamas fresh out of the dryer: she liked to press them to her cheek. Elizabeth felt porous: penetrated by warmth. She wanted to lie there all afternoon. She wanted to lie there forever, under the blue sky of August, filling up with sunlight.

But it grew too hot, and Elizabeth sat up, a little restless.

"I don't know about you people, but I'm going down for a swim."

Her father seemed to come awake. For a moment he had a dazed look before his dark-blue eyes sharpened to alertness. "You go right ahead. I'm content to sit here in lizardly contentment. Lil? Bess is going for a swim."

Her mother murmured something, half asleep, and Elizabeth, placing her hand on her father's arm, shook her head: don't disturb her.

"You be careful," Mrs. Halstrom anyway said, half-sitting up with a worried look and shaking back her hair. They were none of them good swimmers. Elizabeth smiled. "I'm just going in for a wade. The tide's out anyway."

She stood up, feeling heavy with sun. Conscious for a moment of eyes on her, she strolled down toward the shallow greenish water. The sand was silky and scalding hot. He had said "content" and "contentment": not a good sentence. He had not been fully awake. A man with a little mustache looked hard at her as she passed and Elizabeth felt pleased to draw his gaze. Then she felt angry at herself for feeling pleased. Who cared what some nasty little man thought of her? Let him rot. Let him die. But she was pleased anyway. The woman beside the man was thin and wore a red bikini. Elizabeth had a grudge against thin women in bikinis. She was a little heavier than you were supposed to be. She even knew the word for herself: buxom. She had known it at twelve. Skinniness was in fashion, so what could she do? She had big bones; she took after her mother. Her wrists were big. If she starved herself she would look awful. Flesh was no longer allowed, except in discreet doses. If your hipbones didn't stick out you were through. You might as well lay down and die. Of course there were exceptions. Elizabeth knew she had a good figure. She wore a two-piece suit but not a bikini. Those were her phrases: good figure, and buxom. Another was: a woman with a little flesh on her. Her father had once said to her in Howland's, "I like a woman with a little flesh on her." And he had looked at her admiringly. One of the two boys she had slept with, before renouncing promiscuity, had said to her, "You do that well." She hadn't done anything at all, but suddenly she was a girl who did that well. But he had looked pleased with himself, saying it. She had decided not to believe him, except slightly. She wondered if all women carried around their little phrases. Handsome, though not beautiful. Small breasts, but nice legs. A really warm person. A good cook. She does it well. She certainly wasn't fat, or even plump: just plain buxom. And she had a good figure. Men looked at her. And she was not a virgin. On her bad days she could look herself in the eye and say: well, at least you're not a virgin. It didn't help at all: but still. She supposed it was some sort of accomplishment. But she was fussy about falling in love. Men without charm, brilliance, and spiritual perfection need not apply.

Suddenly she thought: Not lay down, but lie down.

The green-brown water between the beach and the sandbar was warm. Elizabeth turned and waved at her parents, who were watching her from the blanket. The nasty little man was also watching. Her mother was sitting in the chair again. Yes, watch me. Watch over me. Because one day it will be too late.

She waded up to her waist and stood for a while, turning her shoulders from side to side and dragging her fingertips along the top of the water. She half-remembered a game of her childhood, and cupping a hand she held it just under the surface. You tried to trap a little spot of sun. It was called a fisheye. She couldn't remember how to do it. It didn't matter, really. Maybe you needed a bit of seaweed. But even the seaweed didn't seem to help. No: there it was. A spot of yellow floating in her palm: a yellow eye. The man had stared at her behind. She hoped he enjoyed it: she had a good one. Men staring at women's behinds. She wished she had an eye back there: then she could wink at them. Just fine, thanks. And you? People standing around half-naked on beaches, looking each other over. Or pretending not to look, to be above it all. Boys looking over girls, girls looking over boys. But the real killer: girls looking at girls, women at women. It was the cruellest look she knew. A look of hungry, harsh appraisal. Her this is too that. Mine is bigger. Hers is better. One day she and Marcia had invented a wonderful new bathing suit. It would cover all the parts of the body left uncovered by old-fashioned bikinis, and expose all parts now covered. They called it the Negative Bikini. It was revolutionary. It was worth a fortune. It cracked her up.

Elizabeth waded out to the sandbar and walked along the wet dark shine to the firmer sand in the middle. A fat little girl was sitting in the mud, spreading it carefully over her arms. Even she was wearing a bikini. Two boys raced; the sound of their feet on the solid wet sand was beautiful. It sounded like softly clapping hands. Beyond the sandbar people were swimming; the water was breast-high. Elizabeth waded out and went for a little swim. She swam poorly, but at least she knew how to swim. She had never been much of a beach person. She wanted to get her hair wet, she wanted to be wet all over. She wanted to dry out in the sun.

She came back up the beach toward the blanket, glancing at the woman in the red bikini as she passed. The man lay on his stomach, his face turned away.

Elizabeth stood dripping on the blanket; water streamed from her hair. She rubbed her head hard with the towel.

"Here, Dad," she said, and flicked waterdrops at him, laughing.

"Don't do that," he said sharply, jerking his face away.

"Did you have a good swim?" said her mother. "It's such a lovely day."

Elizabeth lay down in the sun. Farther up the beach, where a few scraggly trees grew in the sand, some boys were throwing a baseball back and forth. The smack of the baseball in the leather gloves, the shouts of children, the low waves breaking slowly in uneven lines and drawing back along the sand, soothed her like soft music. A faint tang of saltwater rose from her skin. She smelled delicious to herself. Her father had wounded her for no reason. A sharp word was a knife. She lay grieving in the sun.

Dr. Halstrom said, "The tide seems to be coming in now, if I'm not mistaken. It's a good thing we didn't lay our blankets down by the water. We saw you bending over in the water, Bess. Were you looking for something?"

Then it was nothing. She was too emotional. Excessive.

"No. Yes, in a way. I was trying to make fisheyes: you know, those spots of sunlight? I did it, too."

"You used to think you could bring them back," he said. "You tried to bring me one, once."

"Oh, come on. I don't remember that. Really?"

"Absolutely. You thought they were pieces of gold. You kept holding the water in your hands and running up the beach. But when you arrived it was all gone."

"It sounds a little sad." She felt sad. The poor child! Gold running through her fingers.

"Not at all. It was a generous, noble, and beautiful thing to have done. Your mother and I were extremely touched. I explained to you that it was sunlight, and not gold, but that in another sense, a more important sense, it was gold, and that you had accomplished what you set out to do."

Elizabeth felt so full of love for this man, this father, who gravely called her noble and generous, that she knew she could only disappoint him. She was bound to let him down, in the long run. She felt that if he knew the truth about her he would never forgive her. And yet she had no particular truth in mind. It was just how she felt.

"A fine mouthful for a five-year-old child," said Mrs. Halstrom. "Poor Bess! She didn't know whether she was coming or going."

"I'm certain she understood what I said to her." As if aware of the sharpness he added, "Or else she pretended to." He laughed. "But that would have been nobler still."

It was an absolutely perfectly lovely day. The sun burned down, the baseball made smacking noises. The sun warmed her clear through, filled her with lazy golden warmth. She was a golden girl, lying in the sun. She thought of the slow barge lazily sunning itself like a great lazy cat of a barge, stretching out its great barge-paws, slowly closing its drowsy barge-eyes. Beside her she heard her father take up a book. The turning of a page was a beautiful sound. Under the hot blue sky Elizabeth felt a pleasant drowsiness. She felt more and more relaxed, as if some tightness were flowing out of her. She felt calm and clear as a glass of water. A page turned. The turning of a page was like a low wave falling. The sun shone down. To fall asleep in the sun.

Elizabeth seemed to start awake. "Good gracious!" It was her mother's voice. Her father was staring at the water with lips drawn tight. Elizabeth sat up and saw.

A boy who looked about sixteen was walking along the beach down by the water. He wore heavy bootlike shoes, black denims, and a dark, heavy parka fastened up to his neck. His hands were thrust so hard in his coat pockets that he seemed to be tugging down his shoulders. He walked quickly, furiously. Sweat streamed along his dark-tanned cheeks. He had black hair and black furious eyes. His face was so taut with fury that his high sharp cheekbones seemed to be pushing through the skin. His tense tugged-down walk made him look as if he were holding himself tightly in place to keep from blowing apart. His black eyes looked as if a black bottle had exploded inside him and flung two sharp pieces of glass into his eyeholes.

"Imagine," said Mrs. Halstrom, "wearing a coat like that in weather like this. What on earth do you suppose is wrong with him?"

"Don't encourage him with your attention," said Dr. Halstrom, turning a page harshly.

All along the beach people turned to look at the dark parka. The boy tramped with hard angry strides along the firm wet sand at the edge of the beach. Water slid over his boot-toes but he tramped splashing on the water, indifferent, wrapped in his rage. Sweat glistened on his dark cheeks. Two girls on a blanket exchanged smiles. A little girl in the water pointed at him and yelled with excitement. On a blanket crowded with teenagers a muscular boy in tight turquoise-blue trunks stood up with his fists on his hips, but did not move or speak.

Down by the water the boy in the parka tramped past. For a moment his furious black gaze swept the beach. Elizabeth saw his lips draw back in mockery, in disdain.

"Don't stare at him," said Dr. Halstrom.

"I'm not staring at him," said Elizabeth, startled; angry. She was furious. Blood beat in her neck.

"It only serves to attract his attention."

And suddenly an extraordinary thing happened. The furious boy reached back over his shoulders and put up his hood. He plunged his hands back in his pockets and stared out of his hood with black broken-glass eyes, mocking and furious. Sweat poured along his face and shone in the sun. He tramped past. Rage consumed Elizabeth. She was a black flame. She felt the hood over her head, she tramped on waves. Sweat poured down her cheeks. Sun-people on beaches: laughter in the sun. Glittering people on beaches laughing. She swept them with her furious black gaze. The beach glittered in the sun. Hate welled in her heart. It was all a lie. Out with the sun! People on beaches caught up in the lie of the sun. Deniers! She mocked them. She trampled the water. Hate raged in human hearts. The beach lied. She was alone in the dark.

"Beach like that." Elizabeth was startled into her skin by her mother's voice. Her heart was beating quickly, she felt a little faint. Sweat trickled along her neck.

"I find the entire subject—" her father was saying.

The dark, hooded figure was far down the beach. People lost interest in him as he moved farther away. The excited little girl was sitting down in the water, splashing about and laughing. Far down the beach he seemed a small, dark animal on a brilliant expanse of snow.

"But why would anyone behave like that?" said Mrs. Halstrom.

"He wished to attract as much attention as possible and he succeeded admirably. The subject is not interesting."

When he reached the jetty he leaped up onto a rock and looked back at them: he was so far away that Elizabeth could no longer see his face. Then he climbed to the path at the top of the jetty and strode toward the parking lot. He was gone.

"I hope you locked the car," said Mrs. Halstrom, turning her head and shading her eyes.

"The parking lot is policed. I suggest we drop the subject."

"But why on earth," said Mrs. Halstrom, still shading her eyes.

"He was clearly disturbed. I asked you to drop the subject."

"I never saw anything like it. Never."

"I said drop it."

"He was mocking us," said Elizabeth.

Dr. Halstrom turned to her angrily. "Just what do you suppose you mean by that?"

"There's no call to be angry," said Mrs. Halstrom.

Dr. Halstrom closed his book. "Well, my day is ruined by

this constant squabbling." His eyes were blue fire. Elizabeth felt tired.

"I meant he was mocking us—them—all this." She raised her arm and made a slow, sweeping gesture, including the sand, the water, and the sky. For a moment she looked at her arm held gracefully against the sky. Far out on the water the barge had moved on, quite a distance.

"All this? I trust you can be a little more articulate."

"All of it." She dropped her arm. She looked at her hand lying on the blanket. "He was protesting." It was impossible to go on. "Against all this. Against the sun." She was a fool. She had no words. She felt drained.

"Good heavens, Bess," said Mrs. Halstrom.

"Protesting against the sun, eh?" Elizabeth looked up. His voice was no longer angry. She didn't understand anything. "Well by God he didn't succeed very well." He pointed. "It's still there, I notice."

"What a conversation," said Mrs. Halstrom. She began to comb her hair.

"Though if it comes to that, I confess I agree with him. It's hot as blazes."

He laughed lightly, at ease, showing his boyish smile with the two handsome hollows like elongated dimples.

"Why don't you take a little dip, if you're hot?" said Mrs. Halstrom. "It's a good time of day." She pulled the comb slowly through her dark sunshiny hair.

"Your hair is so lovely," Elizabeth said.

"Why, thank you, Bess." She stopped combing. "What a dear thing to say. Yours is too."

A line of low waves fell gray and green and white along the far edge of the sandbar. Low slow water fringed with white slid lazily forward, stopped in different places, and silkily slipped back. A little girl in a brilliant yellow bathing suit stood looking down at her feet.

"Oh, Daddy," said Elizabeth suddenly, leaning back on the warm blanket and stretching out her arms along her sides, "do you know I can't even remember what brand of bread it was? Isn't that awful?"

"The tide's coming in," said Mrs. Halstrom, shaking out her hair. "You'll feel much better, after a dip."

"Silvercup," said Dr. Halstrom decisively.

The Sledding Party

Catherine discovered that it was really two parties. The indoor party took place in the warm, lamplit playroom, with its out-of-tune piano that did not quite conceal a folded-up ping-pong table, and the outdoor party took place on the snowy slope of the Anderson back yard. From the top of the slope you could look down across the floodlit driveway to the dark, open garage at the side of the house. Under the floodlight the snow-lumped bushes, glazed and glistening, looked like crusted pastries with rich, soft centers. Now and then the inner door leading to the playroom would open, and there would come a burst of voices, laughter, and rock-and-roll, followed by sudden silence. A few moments later a shadowy, winter-coated figure would step from the garage into the glare of the floodlight, revealing itself to be Linda Shulick or Karen Soltis or Bill Newmeyer or Roger Murray or anyone else who might want to leave the hot crowded room and come into the fresh winter night. The figure would cross the driveway, trudge up the hill, and join the group beside the willow for a smoke in the cold air or a ride down the path in the snow. The good thing about two parties was that you could pass back and forth between them. You never felt trapped.

The sledding path itself was simply a wonder. The path began at the top of the slope, beside the willow, and after a sweeping curve it headed sharply down. Then came a second, lesser curve, and a little more than halfway down, the path forked abruptly. You could steer to the right and continue down to the high snow and half-buried hedge near the bottom of the driveway, or you could steer to the left and pass the wild cherry and end up in the high snow near the mountain laurel in the flat part of the yard. From the bottom of the path you could look up at the yellow windows of the playroom. To everyone who arrived, Len Anderson explained that he and his father had shoveled the path all that day; and after dinner, when the temperature had fallen to twenty-six, Len had carried out pot after pot of water, coating the path carefully with a layer of ice. That was to ensure maximum speed. Mr. Anderson was a mechanical engineer, and Len always said things like "maximum efficiency" and "ensure maximum speed." But Catherine thought it was a lovely path anyway. The snow on both sides was a foot and a half deep.

A new white Studebaker turned into the driveway, and at the same time, from the bottom of the hill, came shouts and laughter: Bob Carwin and Bonnie Baker tumbling into the snow. "Hey, Bobby boy, none of that, now!" "He did that on purpose." The night sky was a rich, dark blue. It seemed to Catherine, taking deep breaths, that she smelled the richness and freshness of the dark-blue winter night. She wondered whether it was possible to know a winter night by its smell, the way you could know a summer night or an autumn night by its smell. The Studebaker stopped at the top of the drive, and under the floodlight Sonia Holmes got out. Perhaps it was possible to smell snow. It would be a white, cool, fresh smell, like the smell of a cool white sheet. Or was snow simply an absence of smell: of the sharp green aroma of grass, the faintly acrid smell of moist earth? Bev Carlotti came over to Catherine. "I can't believe it. Do you see what she's wearing?" Sonia Holmes went into the garage.

Roger said, "Have you seen my sled? I left it against the tree. It's gone."

"Oh, look!" said Catherine. She was stunned. "Was that a rabbit?" A little animal had gone hobbling across the dark upper yard.

"A cat, I think," someone said.

"A rat," someone else said.

"A skirt to go sledding in. Nylons; the whole bit. She kills me. She's probably wearing heels. I suppose she thinks it's the spring dance."

"Well," said Brad, "at least she didn't come in a bathing suit."

"Don't bet on it. She gives me a swift pain I hate to say where. She ought to wear a sign on her chest: Look on my works, ye Mighty, and despair."

"It didn't look like a cat," said Catherine. "Unless cats hop. Cats don't, do they?"

"They might," said Roger, "in the snow. They might have to. Someone stole my sled. This isn't a bad party. At least they let you smoke."

"You sound like my father," said Catherine. "This party is not unwonderful."

"This party," said Roger, "is very unbad."

Sonia Holmes had come to the sledding party wearing nylons. Catherine imagined her long, sleek legs glittering in the moonlight as she sledded down the path, under the dark, rich-blue sky. It seemed festive. Why not?

"Maybe she isn't planning to go sledding," said Brad. "I hope she is, though. It might be worth watching—especially if she falls off."

"I bet she came to the wrong party," said Bev. "Whoops, 'scuse me, folks. I just stopped by to use your convenience. Can someone point the way to the powder room? Cath, what on earth are you doing?"

"I was looking at the moon. My eyes were closed because I was trying to see if I could tell whether the moon was out even if my eyes were closed. Parties make me feel a little insane. Listen, here's what we'll do. We'll call Mr. Holmes. Mr. Holmes, a dreadful accident has occurred. Mr. Holmes, I regret to inform you that your daughter has lost her pants. She's hiding in the cellar, Mr. Holmes. Mr. Holmes, I know we can trust you to be discreet."

"Well, could you?" said Roger.

"What are you talking about?"

"The moon. You said you were trying to tell if the moon— welcome, stranger."

"Ride down with me, Cath?" It was Peter Schiller, holding a sled.

"Sure. But let me steer, all right? Listen, do you know what Bev said? She said Sonia ought to wear a sign around her chest: Look on my works, ye Mighty, and despair."

"Ozymandias," said Peter.

Catherine looked away in sharp irritation.

"She came in a skirt and stockings," he said.

"We know."

"But you don't know what she said. When she came into the room Helen said to her, 'Are you going sledding like *that?*' She gave Helen one of her Sonia looks and said, 'I didn't think you *had* to go.' That was how she said it: 'I didn't think you *had* to go.' " Peter laughed. "Well, come on. Have you done it with two before?"

"Not exactly."

He put down the sled. "Well, it's a little tricky." He bent over the sled, pushed it lightly to the start of the path, and lay down. He looked over his shoulder. "Just think of me as a sled. Try not to get off center. I can't steer much with my hands on the inside, but I can help a little. It's better to get a running start, but we'll ask Brad to push us off this time. O.K.?"

"I'll just think of you as a sled, Peter." As she said it, laughing, Catherine was startled at the cruel and mocking sound of her words, but no one seemed to notice. Peter lay on the sled in his heavy coat and tucked-in scarf. She lay down on top of him, shifted about, and grasped the outside of the steering bar. She felt awfully high up. Her boots kept sliding off his legs. "Put your feet on the sled, Cath, it's safer. O.K., Brad. Give us a push. Easy." Brad bent over them and eased them forward along the flat start of the path. He gave a light push and released them.

Catherine steered clumsily around the curve and felt herself slipping to one side, but she managed to stay on as they swung onto the downward path. The runners rushed over the glazed snow, and she felt herself still slipping to one side as they took the second curve and came to the fork. She turned sharply to the left, rocking the sled and feeling a boot drag against the snowbank. She jerked to the right, and suddenly they were rushing at the right bank; Catherine braced herself, but somehow they were back on the path. Half on and half off, they rushed past the wild cherry and came to an abrupt stop in the high snow. Catherine fell off. "Damn." She burst into laughter, lying on her back in the snow. The sky was dark, radiant blue. The moon was so bright that it seemed lit from within. It reminded her of the eye of a great cat. The night was a dark-blue cat with a mad moon eye. Snow burned on her cheeks and a soft powder of snow stirred in the air about her. She could feel a coil of hair on her snow-wet cheek. She stretched out her arms and began moving them back and forth in the snow, as if she were giving semaphore signals. Peter stared down at her. "You'd better get up, Cath. What are you doing?" "Snow-angels. Didn't you ever do that as a kid?" He stared down at her and she burst out laughing. "Oh, Peter, you look so bewildered!" She stood up, dusting off snow.

They trudged uphill, Peter's buckled boots jangling.

The second time it went much better: Catherine took the first curve smoothly, swung effortlessly onto the left fork, steered past the wild cherry, and never once felt herself slipping. She drove into their tracks beside the blurred snow-angel, and brought them to a stop five feet beyond their first mark.

She was exhilarated as they walked uphill. "Isn't there something festive about snow? Festive and solemn. I can't explain it. Oh, I can. It's festive because it turns everything into odd shapes, and solemn because it's white, like nurses, and hushed, and very smooth and formal, like a linen table-cloth."

Peter laughed. "That's wild. Have you got your scores back yet?"

"Not yet. Brad got 787 in Math."

"Well, he can always join the Army."

"He had to break the news gently to his mother. I hear Sonia got an 800 in posture."

Peter burst into loud, nervous laughter.

The third time, it was Peter's turn. Catherine lay on the sled and grasped the inside of the steering bar. "Watch out for that tree, Peter. Remember old Ethan Frome." He pushed the sled, running behind as he bent over it, then threw himself lightly and easily on top of her as he took the outside of the steering bar. She could feel his chin pressing into her thick fur collar. They went much faster, took the curves well, rushed into the left fork, and flew past the wild cherry. At the bottom they came to a halt a few feet past their second mark—a record every time. She felt Peter moving her hair and kerchief away from her ear, and she heard him say "Love you" or "I love you." She stayed very still. Nothing happened. All at once the weight left her body; she heard the jangle of boot buckles and a sharp crunch of snow.

When she was sure he was going away she looked over her shoulder and saw him walking across the driveway toward the garage.

Catherine dragged the sled up the hill and stood beside the willow. He had moved away her hair and said those words. She felt violated, betrayed.

Brad came over. "What happened to Peter?"

"Nothing. He got cold, I guess."

"Would you care for company on the downward path to ruin?"

"Not now, Brad. I've had it, for a while."

"Where's Peter?" asked Bev.

"God, Peter Peter Peter. He just went inside. What's all the commotion about?"

"Nothing. You're standing there with his sled."

"That is not a sled," said Brad. "It is Peter, bewitched. Let us honor the memory of our late friend, Miss Carlotti, by sharing a ride."

Catherine handed him the sled and walked through the soft, hanging twigs of the willow into the snowy flatness of the upper yard. Her red galoshes, black-red in the moonlight, sank almost to their furred tops. The black twig-ends of some buried bush stuck up out of the snow; a small withered leaf still clung to one of the twigs, and shook slightly. The sight of the trembling leaf disturbed Catherine, and she looked away. She came to a tall, broad pine that leaned to one side, as if it had begun to fall but had changed its mind. The long lower branches, heavy with clumps of snow, grew close to the ground. A few of the branches had been broken off, leaving an open space.

Catherine bent over and entered the prickly shelter of the tree. The outer parts of the branches were heavy with snow, but toward the trunk the branches showed their bark. She dusted off the bark of a thick branch and sat down, leaning back against the trunk and laying one leg along the branch. Through black and snowy pine-needles she could see the crowd by the willow, the bottom of the sledding path, and the open, dark garage.

It was not possible that Peter Schiller had said those words. It was so impossible that she wondered whether he had said something else, something that sounded like it. She tried to think of something that sounded like it, and began going through the alphabet: above, dove, glove—remembering, at "glove," that in the ninth grade she had written an awful sonnet just that way, and wondering what had ever happened to that sonnet. Was it in the attic? Maybe he had said "I'm above you" or "A glove for you." But she knew perfectly well what he had said. And he had walked away. He had said it and walked away. He had no right. And he knew it: he was ashamed. She and Peter Schiller were friends, they had been good friends for more than three years, but if they were good friends it was precisely because there was nothing more to it than that. She had never thought of him in that way. He was sweet, and irritating, and she could almost be herself with him; she liked to tease him about his horrible French pronunciation, and he had once written a limerick beginning "There was a young lady called Cath, Who was better at English than Math." They were comrades. They hit it off. Catherine knew she had a playfulness about her, even a flirtatiousness, and she needed friends who were playful as well as intelligent. In the auditorium, where members of the National Honor Society were allowed to sit after lunch, she enjoyed a sense of light-heartedness, of pleasurable release from the routines and responsibilities of school, and not everyone rose to the occasion as Peter Schiller sometimes did. The fact was, they got on well together; and that was all. He was not her type. No one was her type. She had ridden down with him on the sled because he had asked her, but she would have ridden down with Brad or Roger or even Bill Newmeyer. They were all friends.

He had moved away her hair and whispered it. She had felt his finger on her ear. Suddenly she realized that he must have removed his glove. He had trapped her on the sled and said it.

Catherine heard a jangle of boot buckles; her stomach tightened, as if she were about to be punched. She wanted to run away, over the snow, into the sky, beyond the moon, but it was only Brad. He looked in at her, bending over and resting his gloved hands, leather and wool, on his knees. Bits of snow clung to his thick orange scarf, and a thread of snow hung from one eyebrow.

"Is anything wrong?"

"No, I'm just sitting here." She gave a shrug and hugged herself. "I like it here. Did you make it down?"

"I think we went through the tree and came out the other side, but other than that. You're sure nothing's wrong?"

"I like watching from here. You have snow on your eyebrow. No, now it's worse. You have snow on your glove."

When he left, Catherine felt forlorn. Forlorn! The very word was like a bell. She was sitting alone in a cold tree, and everyone else was laughing, and sledding, and running up and down hills. He had said it, and there was no way he could unsay it. Catherine had vaguely expected to hear those words someday, just as she vaguely expected to hear "Will you marry me?"—she felt it was inevitable, there was no way around it— but they would be uttered by someone she could not even imagine. They had nothing whatever to do with anyone she knew, or with this town, or with this life. When she heard them, she would be somewhere else. She would not even be herself.

He had looked down strangely at her, lying in the snow. Now she would never know what he was thinking. She could never trust him. She wondered whether he had felt that way all of a sudden, or whether he had been feeling that way a long time. Once, in sophomore year, he had drawn a heart in the black wax of her dissecting pan. It had been a frog's heart, with labels like PULMONARY VEINS and RIGHT AURICLE. He had drawn a feathered arrow going through it.

"Hey, are you all right?"

Catherine started; she had not heard Bev come up.

"Yes, I'm fine, I'm fine. What's wrong with everybody tonight?"

"You're sitting in a tree, Cath. Nobody else is sitting in a tree."

"Well, I believe in Nature. I believe Americans ought to

get back to Nature, like the Indians. God, can't a poor working girl enjoy Nature without everybody having a conniption
fit? Slaving in the factory nine to five, six days a week, ten
children, my husband drunk every night—"

"Hell, honey, you think you got problems. My husband
don't drink, but I got ten drunk children. Listen, a bunch of
us are going inside now, O.K.? I've had enough of Mother
Nature for one night. Time to catch a little of the Sonia
Holmes show. They've got Potato Frills, Cath. Suit yourself. I
tried."

Catherine watched them tramp down to the driveway and
into the garage. The inner door opened, and she heard shouts
and laughter and music: piano chords, not records. Only
Roger and Bill Newmeyer stayed outside, sledding hard, over
and over again, with a concentration and seriousness that
seemed to her beautiful. Someone smoking a cigarette came
up from the house—it was George Silko—and joined them
for a time, but the spirit of pure, silent concentration had
been broken, and soon all three went down to the house.
Catherine was alone, in her tree.

She could never go down there, because Peter Schiller was
there. He had pinned her to the sled and put those words
inside her, and then he had gone back to the house and left
her there with the words inside. It was as if—she tried to think
how it was—he had suddenly touched her breast. She felt he
had delicately wounded her in some way.

A light went on over the garage: the party had spread to the
kitchen. Through a sliver of window between translucent curtains she saw someone pass clearly between blur and blur.
Down in the playroom someone must have opened a window,
for Catherine could hear the out-of-tune piano coming from
the front of the house. A voice cried "I can't find it." There
was a burst of laughter. The window shut.

For a moment she had been drawn into the warm room and the laughter, and now she was banished to her cold tree. She remembered standing at the top of the slope, feeling the moonlight pour into her face. It seemed a long time ago. Catherine felt that something strange was happening, that at any moment the house below might start slowly sliding away over the snow, like a great, silent ship with yellow windows.

She heard the piano again: someone was coming to get her. From the garage Len Anderson, wearing a sweater but no coat, stepped onto the driveway. He had his hands in his pockets, and he hunched his shoulders quickly against the cold. He looked up at the willow, and then at the pine, and walked rapidly across the driveway, stopping at the side of the hill. "Catherine?" he called. She wondered if he could see her through the dark branches. "Here," she answered, feeling absurd. Len raised an arm and waved. "O.K.!" he said, and turned around and went back into the house.

She supposed they were all talking about her. Where was Catherine? Sitting in a stupid tree. Everything was strange, all the houses were about to float away, the moon was looking sorrowfully for Catherine, but no one was there.

She hugged herself in the cold, shivered dramatically, as if someone were watching, and tried to understand what had happened. She had been in one of her moods, wide open to the blue mystery of night and the festive, solemn snow. There were times when the world seemed to Catherine a whole series of little explosions, going off one after the other, and all she could do was stand transfixed, feeling it happening all around her. And so they had ridden down on the sled, and she had lain on her back in the snow, looking up at Peter Schiller's bewildered face. And perhaps, without intending to, she had encouraged him to say those words. She had caught him in her wonder. She had bewitched him. She had offered herself to the night and the snow, and poor old Peter had misunderstood. It wasn't his fault. And the longer she stayed in her tree, the more awkward everything was becoming. It seemed to her that she must go down to the house quickly, quickly, and set things right. She would behave as if nothing had happened. And then, in a moment when they were alone, she would explain that she had been touched by what he had said—really touched, Peter—but that she preferred to think of him as a dear friend. She hoped he would think of her that way too. She was not in love with anyone at all.

Catherine was so relieved that she clapped her gloved hands, sending up a faint snowspray. She felt that if she could see him quickly, and explain, then the words would go away, as if they had never been spoken. Everything would be all right between them. Nothing would have happened at all.

Catherine tried to hurry through the high snow. She had to take big, awkward steps, and snow got into her boots. She thought of the rabbit or cat she had seen at the back of the house. She wondered if it had found a warm, dry place, out of the snow. On the driveway she looked down at the little mounds of snow on her boot-toes and stamped each foot hard. As she entered the garage and passed along the side of a darkly gleaming car, a nervousness came over her, but she hurried on.

The inner door opened onto a tiny hall. Wooden steps covered with black rubber led up to the kitchen. Directly on her left was the dark-red door of the playroom. On her right was a dusky workroom where, on a long workbench under a dim yellow bulb, dripping coats lay carelessly heaped.

"The mystery woman returns," said Brad from the couch. He gave a little wave. The room was hot and dimly lit and full of smoke. She did not see Peter. She felt her cheeks tightening and tingling in the warmth, as if her face were being pulled carefully into place over her skull. Ned Toomey, seated at the piano with a cigarette in the corner of his mouth and his eyes narrowed in the upstreaming smoke, was playing "Sloop John B." Beside him, looking intensely at the music and holding in one outstretched hand an empty glass, stood Richie Jelenik, singing in a deep, mournful voice. On the other side Ken Jackson stood with one foot on the piano bench, playing the guitar and leaning close to the music as he looked back and forth quickly from the notes to his left hand. The two couches were full, people walked about, on the floor in a lamplit corner Roger and Bill Newmeyer were building a high tower with small colored blocks. "They said you were in a tree," said Nancy Russell, and Catherine noticed that Nancy Russell's eyebrows were not the same length. A bowl of Potato Frills appeared. A hand held out a paper cup of ginger ale. Catherine, glancing at a window, saw with surprise her surprised face. Through herself she saw brilliant yellowish snow and a yellow-lit lantern on a black pole. Ned Toomey and Ken Jackson came to the end of "Sloop John B," and Richie Jelenik put his glass down on the piano. They began to play "Goodnight Irene." Catherine moved across the room toward Brad. "I'm back," she said, and sat down next to him as he shoved over. "Isn't it awfully smoky in here?"

"It goes with the décor. We can have a tree brought in for you, if you'd like that. We could set it up by the piano."

"I had a wonderful time in my tree, thanks. All it needed was a heater. Where's Bev?"

"Upstairs, enjoying the absence of smoke, music, and teen-age fun."

"I guess Peter fled up there too."

"I don't know. He was here when we came in, moping in that corner. I thought he went out again. What did you say to him, cruel woman? Oh, they're good at this one."

Ned Toomey had broken off "Goodnight Irene" and had passed without pause into a series of climbing, suspenseful phrases with his right hand. There were shouts of applause. The phrases climaxed in harsh rock-and-roll chords, and Richie Jelenik sang deeply, soulfully, soaringly:

"Ah
Found
Mah
Thri-hill"

"Louder!" cried Brad. "Sing it, Richie babe!"

"Own bluebayry hih-ill"

"Go, Ned!"

"Own bluebayry hih-ill"

"These guys are too much." Richie Jelenik's eyes were closed, his head flung back, his face twisted in a parody of passion; and the tense fingers of his outstretched hands were hooked like claws. His cheek glistened, and Catherine was shocked: she thought he was crying. But she saw that he was sweating in the close, warm air. All at once she saw a bright green hill, covered with tall trees, ripe blueberry bushes, and winding paths. Sunlight streamed in through the leaves and fell in shafts onto the lovely paths; and all was still and peaceful in the blue summer air. It was as if the world were waiting for something, waiting and waiting with held breath for something that was bound to happen, but not yet, not yet. Suddenly Catherine felt like bursting into tears. She looked about. Her temples throbbed in the smoke-filled air; she felt a little sick. "I think I'll go up and say hello to Bev," she said.

"Tell her to come on down and join the party. These guys are terrific."

Catherine escaped from the room and climbed the wooden stairs toward the kitchen. On her left at the top of the stairs was the dark, moonlit living room, glowing like an enchanted cave filled with chests of precious jewels. You were not allowed to go into the Anderson living room. In the bright-yellow kitchen to her right, Bev was standing at the stove, gently shaking a black frying pan containing dark-yellow corn kernels. She thrust a large potcover over it and shook harder. Sue Wilson, Linda Shulick, and Joey Musante were sitting at the kitchen table. On the table stood a large bottle of 7Up, a bowl containing crumbs of popcorn, and a smaller bowl filled with thin straight pretzels. Catherine went over to Bev and, leaning close to her ear, said, "Boo." Bev gave a little start. "God, you scared me. I thought you were hibernating for the winter. Do you know, Len thought you were angry at him? Come on, you guys, pop." "Oh no, no. That's crazy. Len?" Through a door in the kitchen Catherine saw the small dim den, crowded with people. Sonia Holmes sat on a couch surrounded by her courtiers. Her glittering legs were tucked under her skirt. You could not smoke in the den or kitchen, you could not play music in the den, you could not drink beer, and you could not set foot in the living room. You could use the top of the stove but not the inside. "It's so hot down there," Catherine continued. "Have you seen Peter around?"

"Peter? You and Peter are some pair."

Catherine drew back her face sharply, as if she had been struck on the cheek. "Oh?"

"You go sit in a tree, and Peter goes home."

"Peter went home?"

Sue Wilson said, "He didn't even tell anybody. Janet saw him. She thought he went to get something in his car, but he got in and drove away. I call that rude."

Bev said, "Peter isn't rude."

"He left his sled," said Catherine. A restlessness came over her, and she thought how irritating and boring all these people were, and this kitchen, and this universe, and above all, above all, those little straight pretzels. Why weren't they the three-ring kind?

"It's about time!" said Bev. She tipped up the cover and Catherine saw a kernel burst into flower. Bev banged the cover down and shook the pan; there was a crack-crack-cracking. Catherine went over to the den and looked in quickly. Then she turned, walked across the kitchen, and went downstairs.

Through the half-open door of the playroom Catherine saw drifting smoke and the corner of a couch. She went into the workroom and put on her coat, fumbling with the plump buttons, shaped like half-globes. Pulling on her boots, and tying her kerchief under her chin, she strode through the garage.

When she stepped outside she saw that some of the party had returned to the slope. She had thought only of escaping from the house, and now she was standing in the floodlight, exposed. She felt like putting her hands over her face. The only private place was the leaning pine. She climbed the slope at the back of the house, away from the sledding path, and headed across the deep snow toward her tree. Under the moon and the dark-blue sky the snow was luminous and tinged with blue.

Catherine stopped; in the open space of the pine she saw Bob Carwin, standing with one arm against the trunk as he leaned over Bonnie Baker, who sat on a low branch. Catherine turned back angrily into the upper yard. There was no place where she could be alone. There were people at the willow, people at the bottom of the sledding path, people in the pine. There were people in the playroom, people in the kitchen, people in the den. The party was spreading; soon it would flow across the yard, over the hedge, and into the next yard. It would flow across the town. It would spread into the dark-blue sky, all the way to the snowy moon.

Catherine stood in the empty upper yard. She felt restless, yet there was no place to go. He had walked to his car and driven home. He had not told anyone he was going home. Catherine thought it was a strange, upsetting thing to have done, and all at once she felt an immense pity for Peter

Schiller, and for herself, as if someone had done something to them and gone away. But it was Peter Schiller who had gone away. Catherine shook her head, as if to shake out the words. She looked about. Everything seemed suspenseful and mysterious—the blue snow, the deep boot-hollows in the snow, the floodlit black of the driveway, startling as spilled ink rushing across a table. It seemed to her that everything she looked at was about to change shape suddenly. But it all remained peaceful, suspended, still. And the sledders rushing down the slope were part of it too, as if their motion were only another form of stillness. A hill of summer blueberries, sledders in the snow. Catherine felt lifted up into stillness, as if things were about to shift slightly, or crack open like kernels, thrusting up inner blossoms. She felt a faint cracking inside her. In another moment she would understand everything. And as she waited, she bowed her head against the cold, as if in prayer.

A shout from the hill startled her. Catherine hugged herself, and shivered in the cold. It had slipped away, whatever it was. She felt tired, as if she had been running for a long time. It seemed to her that she had been set spinning, like a top that travels across a table, touches an object, and, still spinning, rushes off in another direction. The words had set her spinning to the tree, and from there to the playroom, and from there to the kitchen, and from there to the snowy wasteland of the upper yard. And once you were set spinning, who knew where you would stop? She was spinning, spinning, and now she was about to go spinning off again, because she could not bear to be alone. She no longer knew what was going to happen to her. She no longer knew anything at all.

Gravely, her head bowed slightly, Catherine walked down the hill.

But in the glow of the floodlight her spirits revived, and when she stepped into the smoky warmth of the playroom she felt so soothed, so enfolded, that she enjoyed the feel of her own smile as it pushed against her tightening cheeks. Bev and Brad waved from a couch; Catherine waved back. At the piano they were singing "Auld Lang Syne." These were her friends, her dear friends who were waving to her and laughing and playing the piano and singing. There was a clatter of descending footsteps, and Catherine turned to the half-open door. Len Anderson entered, frowning as he lit a cigarette in cupped hands. "You're leaving?" he said, looking up harshly. "Arriving," she answered, and untied her kerchief. "And Len, I can't tell you what a wonderful party it is." Pleasure surged in her; and everyone was surprised when she gave him a big hug.

A Day
in the Country

She had planned to continue further down the slope, but
the slatted red bench in a sun-flooded bend of the path
had proved too great an adventure. It was an adventure
because it was there at all, demanding nothing, feigning indifference, and promising the secret pleasures of truancy.
The wood was warm to her touch. The three hundred pages
of *The Machining of Plastics* in their neatly tied folder remained
unedited at her side, and in the late afternoon light, bright
but no longer hot, Judith continued to look with pleasure
through the opening in the trees at the sunny cliff with its
gazebo of pale, peeled logs, and beyond to the dark green
and light green and blue green of low hills. On the hills lay
darker green patches that slowly moved: the shadows of
clouds. They looked like carelessly strewn dark doilies. A
young woman in faded bluejeans and a crimson T-shirt lay
on her back on the cliff. Her boyfriend sat crosslegged beside
her, drinking a can of beer that flashed in the sun. His shadow
was so richly black that it might have been wet. They spoke,
but quietly, as if hushed by the peacefulness of the view, and
Judith would not have wished them to leave. It struck her,
watching their stillness, that there was also a pleasurable
truancy from play. One of the attractions of the place was its
twenty-seven, or was it twenty-nine, scenic trails, and it was
possible to feel much too responsible for covering the terri-

tory. She had been marching up and down trails all morning and half the afternoon, looking down at valleys with red barns and across at hills with little white houses, identifying fourteen wildflowers with the aid of Peterson's *Field Guide to the Wildflowers of the Northeastern and Central States* and a four-page pamphlet she had bought for ninety-five cents at the gift shop near the dining room, resting only for a few minutes in the rustic gazebos placed along the cliff trails before setting off again, and she realized, seated gratefully on her bench, how delightful it was simply to stop. Simply to stop. At her feet grew a purple wildflower, with four-petaled clusters arranged along the upper part of a thick green stalk, and she purposely refrained from opening her shoulder bag and checking in the purple section of the field guide. The warm sun on her face made her feel healthy and sleepy. Flower, tree, rock, sky—for a moment Judith longed for a world without detail. It would be enough.

She heard footsteps approaching along the upper path and turned to look. A woman, walking slowly, appeared around the bend, and as she did so Judith felt a little sharp burst of annoyance. It was their third encounter of the day. The woman—she couldn't have been more than twenty-seven or -eight, though indoors she looked thirty—was wearing a black sweater and an ankle-length wrap-around in dark blue, with purple and pale-blue swirls. Over her slumped shoulder she wore a large cloth pocketbook with two wide wooden strips at the top; the cloth was dull red with little dark-green leaves all over it. A mane of black hair, lightly clasped at the neck, flowed down to the small of her back. She looked at Judith with large dark melancholy eyes that seemed perpetually to be making a mute appeal, and it was above all those eyes with their mute appeal that irritated Judith, who was suddenly afraid the intruder might want to join her on the bench. Indeed she had almost stopped walking and seemed to be looking tentatively at the unoccupied corner of the small bench, where Judith thanked God she had placed her manuscript and her bag. She was afraid the woman might ask if she could sit down, and then what hope was there? But she only looked again at Judith, who looked severely away. The woman had never quite stopped walking, and she now turned off the main path onto the narrow trail leading to the cliff with the gazebo. She stopped halfway, seeing the lovers, and stood for a few moments looking out at the view with one hand resting on top of her pocketbook. She then turned back and, without a glance at Judith, stepped onto the main path and continued down. Judith's heart was beating quickly; she felt shocked by her own rudeness.

But she couldn't help it. She had first seen her the night before. Judith had left the office at midafternoon on Friday and arrived barely in time for dinner in the great dining hall, with its thirty or forty small square tables and its darkening view of the hills. The long bus ride from Port Authority had tired her, and she had had to wait twenty minutes for the limousine that carried her and four others up the long, winding road to the Mountain Lodge. But as soon as the chateaulike building came into view, sprawling and turreted in all the exuberance of splendidly bad Victorian taste, the little irritations of the trip fell away from her. Her room was at the top of the south wing, in the rear. She had just enough time to drop her suitcase and take in the patchwork quilt in brown and blue and yellow, the dark, curving headboard with pineapple finials, the pale brown wallpaper with pale-pink and pale-green nosegays, and the view of blackening green hills under a fading sunset before hurrying along the carpeted corridor, past window nooks with cushioned seats, to the main stairway, with its thick and glistening banister. From the lobby at the foot of the stairs it was not far to the dining hall at the rear of the north wing. Dinner was served from six to eight, and it was seven-forty-five. Many guests still lingered at their tables, and Judith was pleased: she liked the combination of privacy and company provided by a reserved table in a crowd. It so happened that the tables in her immediate vicinity were

IN THE PENNY ARCADE

unoccupied, except for one a few feet away, and at that table sat a woman with melancholy eyes and a mane of black hair. The absence of other diners nearby had the effect of throwing the two of them into accidental relation, and Judith noticed that she and the younger woman seemed to be the only ones dining alone. It was enough to set her, however unreasonably, against acquaintance. Those melancholy and mutely appealing eyes, which seemed to be seeking a soul mate with whom to share, in hushed tones, in a corner of lamplit darkness, intimate disheartening confessions, were only another reason for keeping between them a decent stretch of spiritual distance. With particular annoyance Judith noted the woman's slumped, defeated shoulders. She longed to say: "Good God, woman, enough. Shoulders back—sit up straight—get a grip on yourself—it can't be as bad as all that. And stop wearing your sorrow like a string of pearls. He isn't worth it. Down with it." She contented herself with studying the menu.

That was the first meeting, if silence and avoidance could in any sense be called a meeting. For Judith it seemed to insist on remaining no less than that. The melancholy woman finished half her slice of pecan pie, lit up a cigarette, and left in a cloud of smoke, without having ventured a syllable. But even the hoped-for silence managed to annoy Judith: it seemed too pointedly a reproach. It was as if it had been up to Judith, who at thirty-six supposed she was the "older woman," to break the silence and launch them into gloomy intimacy. She, however, was planning to enjoy herself for a change. There was a certain kind of exasperating woman who never recovered from the world of the college dormitory, and spent the rest of her life longing for tragic confidences and cozy confessions in an atmosphere of leathery lounges, heaped ashtrays, and crumpled Almond Joy wrappers crackling faintly while the gray of early dawn showed through the many-paned high windows. The dark woman would probably go searching unhappily for that dormitory until doomsday. She ought to get on with it. But Judith's good spirits quickly returned. After dinner she made her way back to the lobby, which led to the front lounge, and when she stepped from the side door into the darkness of the open veranda, she felt something expand within her. She walked to the handrail in front, overlooking the lamplit lake. On three sides the long veranda was built on piles over the water. A wicker chair creaked. Footsteps crunched in the graveled paths beside the lake. In the dark, shining water the reflections of windows broke into ripples of yellow as three ducks, forming a triangle, floated by. On the dry side of the veranda a flight of steps led to a path. Judith crossed the path by the side of the lake and walked partway up the dark hill on the other side. She looked across at the great porch and the tiers of yellow windows, and later, in an armchair in the lamplit lounge, when she sat with *The Machining of Plastics* beside her and the folded *Times* before her and paused over a five-letter word meaning "crest of a mountain," she thought of the dark hill over the lake. The fourth letter was "t." She looked up, as if hoping to find the missing letters in the air before her, and saw the melancholy woman passing slowly across the room. Her dark-green sweater seemed to emphasize her slumped shoulders, her long black skirt hung as if despondently about her, and with the sound of a sigh she exhaled a long stream of swirling smoke while she looked around as if searching for someone who had failed to keep an appointment.

Judith rose early the next morning and came down to breakfast at seven-fifteen in jeans and hiking boots. Her melancholy companion was not there, and Judith had the wickedly pleasurable sense that she would drag herself out of bed with a headache a little before noon. It occurred to Judith that she did not much care for the company of single women; there had been a time when they were her only friends. After breakfast she set off at once along the steepest trail, which still lay in shadow. It led high above the lake to a stone tower with a view. Despite the early hour there were already many strollers on the path, and she smiled at a gray-haired couple whom she recognized from the dining hall. "Fine morning," the man said, touching his fingertips to his temple in a little salute. His blue-eyed wife, whose gray bangs looked like a row of commas, at once remarked vigorously, as if in contradiction: "I think it's a wonderful morning!" Suddenly Judith stepped into the sun. She felt like flinging herself onto the grass at the side of the path, she felt like rolling over and over, but instead she continued climbing. She burst out laughing: she had caught herself humming "Zippity doodah." She wondered when she had last thought of it. With startling vividness she saw Uncle Remus with a bluebird on his shoulder. Judith rested in a sunny gazebo, where she looked down at the long, massive lodge and at the lake, half in sun and half in shade, that stretched along one wing and under the veranda, and then she continued up to the tower. In the bright grass at the foot of the tower six teenagers in patched and faded jeans, three boys and three girls, lay on their backs with their eyes closed. It was windy and their hair moved a little over their immobile sunstruck faces. Judith climbed the winding stone stairs to the top and emerged from a shelter in the center of the round tower. Half a dozen people were already there. At the parapet she looked down at the teenagers, the lake, and the lodge. In the lake a few rowboats were out. She watched one pass from shade to sun. She began to walk slowly round the tower for a view of the valley on the other side, and as she passed into the shadow of the stairway shelter she saw the woman in bright sunlight not ten feet away. She wore a black sweater and a dark-blue wrap-around with pale-blue and purple swirls. She stood conspicuously alone, staring out over the valley with her hands resting on the stone parapet.

Judith made a motion as if to retreat, but stopped herself. It was too silly to sneak away; there was no reason for it. But still she hesitated, wondering whether to stride boldly over and look at the view. The woman remained strangely motionless, and the wild thought struck Judith that she knew she was being observed, knew in fact that Judith was there. But that was mad. The woman moved suddenly, but it was only to lean forward and place her forearms on the parapet, bringing one foot behind the other and balancing it on the toe. Judith stepped to a portion of parapet that did not give the best view of the valley and was separated by a good distance from her solitary companion. She stared fixedly down for what seemed many minutes, gradually leaning forward and placing her arms on the parapet. She became aware of her pose and irritably straightened up. The woman still leaned on the parapet, staring into the distance.

Judith spent the rest of the morning following a long trail that led deep into the wooded hills. Sometimes the trail grew so narrow that the overarching white oaks, beeches, and Norway maples, which she identified with the aid of *A Field Guide to Trees and Shrubs,* shut out all but a few trembling spots of sun. Sometimes it led her to the edges of sun-dazzled, perilous cliffs, where nothing grew but yellowing grass and pink thistles. On one such cliff Judith rested on sun-warmed stone. She stretched out her legs, leaned back on her hands, and lifted her face, with closed eyes, to the sun. The hot mid-morning sun, the richly blue sky, and the distant hills seemed to flow into her and wash her clean, as if she had accumulated an inner grime. When she opened her eyes she saw a white butterfly on her knee.

The trail did not end, but went in a great loop that led back to the lodge. On her return she began to pass more and more people, moving in both directions: the day crowd, already out in force. The noisy crowd irritated her, for it seemed a rude interruption of her peace, but as she came in sight of the great veranda, thronged with visitors, her impa-

tience gave way to a sense of the festive. She was in too good
a humor to spurn the crowd-energy she felt all about her. She
walked along the gravel path at the edge of the lake and
climbed the steps at the side of the veranda. Children ran up
and down the long porch, stopping to lean over the rail and
point at the water. A little girl in a pink dress and black patent-
leather shoes was dragging behind her a clattering yellow
duck on red wheels. A tall, thin, very pale man burst suddenly
into deep, hearty laughter. Through the side door she entered
the sunny lounge, where people strolled back and forth, talking and laughing. She saw the elderly couple that she had
passed early in the morning and gaily waved. When she
entered the dining hall she saw that it was filled, and she
approached her table with a pleasurable sense of proprietor-
ship. Her dark companion had not yet returned for lunch.
In the crowded and lively room Judith felt both soothed and
excited, and she ate hungrily the handsomely served items of
her lunch: a cup of onion soup, slices of small sweet rye and
pumpernickel, a crab salad, and a French pastry so shamefully
sweet that she vowed to hike vigorously all afternoon. But it
felt good to sit lazily over her coffee; her thigh muscles were
a little sore. The table beside her remained empty, and it
seemed to Judith that the woman was deliberately spurning
the crowd—striking an attitude on some lonely cliff.

After lunch Judith sat in a sunny corner of the veranda.
Her long hike had pleasantly tired her, and she was tempted
to sit for hours in the cushioned wicker armchair, feeling the
sun on her arms and face and listening to the sounds about
her: the knock of heels on the wood of the porch, the shouts
of children, the creak of wicker furniture, the opening and
closing of the side door leading to the lounge. The temptation
to remain was so great that she forced herself up, reminding
herself that the next day was her last. Perhaps it would rain.
She followed a trail in the opposite direction from her morning's hike, one that led past the tennis courts and into the
woods. The wooded trail led to a rushing brook; over it was

a shady wooden bridge, flecked with sunlight. Judith stood on the bridge, looking at the bits of sun moving on her hand and at the stones under the clear water. She crossed over and continued on the trail. Here and there wooden benches were placed at the side of the path. A smaller path led off the main trail, and Judith turned into it. It was shady and quiet. The path wound in and out. As Judith rounded a turn, she saw the woman seated on a bench. Judith was so startled that she drew in her breath sharply, and the woman turned to look at her. She had been reading a book, which she continued to hold up in both hands with her arms pressed against her sides as she sat with her head turned a little awkwardly toward Judith, who for a moment, in her surprise and alarm, had come to a full stop. The woman's eyes were melancholy and kind.

"You startled me," Judith said, and broke into stride.

"I hadn't meant to," the other said gently, but Judith was already past.

She hiked in the woods for several hours before deciding to turn back. Her little encounter had upset her, and she hesitated to return along the path that led to the stream. She felt irritated at her hesitation, made up her mind that she didn't care *whom* she passed, and was relieved to discover a new path leading back to the tennis courts. In her room she washed her face and lay down on the sunny bed for five minutes with her arm over her eyes. Then she picked up *The Machining of Plastics* and went down to the veranda. It was far too noisy for her to work. Consulting her map, she decided to take a twisting path that led down through a beech grove and a meadow to a pond. She had not yet come to the beech grove when, suddenly on her right, she saw a red-slatted bench in a sunflooded bend of the path.

The late afternoon sun burned against her face. Judith's sense of pleasurable truancy, disturbed by the woman's appearance and by her own rudeness, did not return. Her present mood eluded her. She felt not so much a restlessness as an unpeacefulness, a dissatisfaction. It was as if a cloud had moved across an inner sun, darkening the green, peaceful, inner hills. The bench was uncomfortably hard, but it was no longer possible to continue down the slope, now that the dark woman had passed that way.

On the cliff the boy set down his flashing beer can. It occurred to Judith that they had chosen that place in order to watch the sunset. All at once, as if he were bowing to the sun, the boy leaned slowly and gracefully over, untucked the girl's crimson T-shirt, and kissed her on the stomach. Judith rose, picked up her manuscript, slung her handbag over her shoulder, and trudged up the trail.

Children, indifferently watched by parents, ran up and down the veranda. A burst of laughter came from one corner: four fat women, all wearing tight pants in pastel shades, were playing cards at a wicker table. Judith passed through the side door into the lounge, where people were walking in every direction. She remembered that tea was served in the dining room at four; perhaps it was not too late, though it was getting on toward half-past. But on the way she decided that she didn't want tea. It wasn't the Isle of Wight, for God's sake. She went up to her room to work until dinner.

Judith felt better for the little work she had done, and on her way down to the dining hall she permitted the charm of the place to cast its spell again. She loved the wide window recesses with their cushioned window seats and the bookshelves on both sides, and she loved the dark, paneled walls hung with glass-covered photographs of the Mountain Lodge at the turn of the century, glass-covered photographs of bearded men in tweed caps and tweed knickerbockers, and glass-covered drawings of herbs and ferns carefully labeled in Latin and English. She loved the broad, thick-carpeted stairway with its sturdy and shiny old banister, whose thick balusters were shaped like bowling pins. She had showered and changed into a rose-colored blouse, beige slacks, and beige sandals, and as she entered the filled and festive dining hall, with its soaring paneled walls and the orange sunset through the tall windows, she felt not merely pleasure but gratitude. The diners, unlike the day crowd, were all here for at least the weekend, sharing the same gentle adventure. The Mountain Lodge was a great ship sailing into the hills, and they were all passengers. She recognized many faces: the tall, very thin man with the hearty laugh, two of the teenagers who had lain on the grass before the tower, the elderly couple who had spoken to her in the morning. They greeted her as she passed; Judith smiled at the woman and, turning to the man, touched the tips of her fingers to her temple. The table beside hers was empty, as were several others here and there in the hall, and when, halfway through dinner, Judith looked up to see the dark woman in her chair, it struck her as being so natural, so entirely without menace or meaning of any kind, that she could have laughed aloud to think of the absurd pains she had taken to evade this harmless creature with the slumped shoulders and melancholy eyes, who had been placed beside her by wildest chance and whom she was not called upon to elude or know. For each to the other was entirely a stranger.

And it was splendid after dinner to sit on the darkening veranda among quiet voices and the sound of creaking wicker. She looked at the sky above hills slowly draining of color. The darkening blue of the east turned to pale, pale blue above, to a blue that was almost white but gave off no light, like a darkness. It was growing cool. "Cheesecloth," a man's voice said decisively, and she tried to hear the next sentence, but his words were interwoven with sounds of footsteps, creaking furniture, a pipe knocking against a glass ashtray. "It's getting a little chilly," a woman said to her husband. A few older men lit up cigars. "I think I'll go in and get my sweater," someone said. "It's this mountain air," someone else said. And all at once, for no reason, the missing letters came to her: arête. The side door opened and closed, someone yawned loudly, people walked on the gravel paths lit by carriage lamps. The veranda smelled of lake water, cigar smoke, and damp wood. It was growing dark.

Someone cried out, then there were gasps and shouts: and the moon, large and fiery orange, rose slowly from the black hills. It was nearly round, except that one side was slightly blurred, as if someone had started to erase it before giving up.

Judith could almost hear the machinery hidden behind the hills, creakily hoisting the cumbrous old moon, which in a moment would probably tumble back down with a crash. But it detached itself from the hill and sat there, looking pleased with itself.

She decided to take a little walk in the lamplit dark before going inside. On the gravel paths by the side of the lake, couples strolled slowly, stopping now and then to look at the water. Judith walked along a path to the other side of the lake and began climbing the dark hill. She had hoped to sit in one of the gazebos on the cliffs along the way, but in each one she passed there sat a couple looking out across the lake. On a stretch of bare flat moon-brightened cliffs, a little distance from the paths, lovers sat and lay as if they were on a beach. Some had brought blankets and lay on their backs, staring up at the night sky. And an irritation came over Judith, at this invasion, this conspiracy of lovers to occupy the best places. The moon had climbed and was pale yellow now. Judith continued up the steep trail, hoping to exhaust the lovers. When she came to the next gazebo she saw a heavy man smoking a pipe, alone. She turned back down the path.

In the warm, lamplit lounge, in an armchair beside one of the big empty fireplaces, Judith sat reading a book about Victorian architecture in New England, which she had found in the small library off the Winter Lounge. In winter there would be fires blazing in all the fireplaces, and suddenly she longed for it to be winter, with logs snapping in the fireplace beside her and, through the bay windows, fields of smooth snow glistening under the moon.

"Hello there." The voice startled her, and she looked up to see the elderly man who had saluted her on the path. His wife, who had spoken, stood beside him.

"Oh, hello," Judith said.

"We saw you sitting here all by your lonesome, and we thought, now why don't we just go over and say hello."

"We saw you reading a book by yourself here. I told Bea, we shouldn't disturb her, if she's reading."

"Oh, that's all right. I'm just sitting here, really. Soaking up the atmosphere."

"Well, that's fine," said the woman. "It's a fine evening. We saw you sitting alone, dear, and we just wanted to come over and say hello. We'll be right across the room there, if you'd care for comp'ny."

The woman pointed across the room. The man bent his head slightly, touched two fingers to his temple, and lifted them. Taking his wife by the arm, he turned and walked with her slowly back across the room.

A warm, tender feeling rose in Judith, as if the word "dear" had been a hand laid on her cheek. A desire came over her to follow the kindly couple across the room, to pull up an armchair beside them and recount the little adventures of her day: the fourteen wildflowers, the climb to the top of the tower, the red bench in the sun, her unedited manuscript, the three ducks in a triangle scattering the yellow windows, the wooden bridge over the stream. Perhaps she could even tell them about the dark woman, and about the beauty and grace of the boy as he bent over the girl. Then they would explain to her what everything meant. And the man would touch his fingers to his temple, and the woman would say:

"That's all right, dear. That's as it should be, dear."

Judith looked up, and saw a plump, bald man with the face of a child, who sat with his knees apart, his plump hands resting on his thighs, and his pants cuffs raised to show red-and-blue argyle socks. She saw a woman with blue-gray hair who sat stiffly upright in her armchair, raising her thin arm to pat gently at her hair while her ivory bracelet slipped slowly from her wrist to her forearm. In an armchair a girl of twenty in tight faded jeans and a burnt-orange sweater sat hugging her raised knees and staring over the tops of them as, flexing and unflexing her bare toes, she listened intensely to a young man with a short blond beard, black-rimmed eyeglasses, and bright-blue eyes. Judith felt that she wanted to tell these people something important, something about how strange it was to be sitting in chairs in a lounge in the middle of the hills, how everything was startling and utterly unknown, how each of them was as wondrous as a giraffe or a rhinoceros, but her thoughts grew confused, the expansive, mysterious feeling passed away, and she saw before her a roomful of dull people, sitting around with nothing to do.

A tiredness came over her, and leaning back for a moment she closed her heavy-lidded eyes. The sun and the hiking had tired her; it had been a long day. It was already past nine. Tomorrow's weather was supposed to be sunny and warm, with highs in the mid-seventies, possibly clouding over in the afternoon. She wanted to be up early: breakfast at six, or say six-thirty at the latest, and out in the sun by seven. She would set her alarm for five-thirty; she could be in bed by half-past nine.

When she opened her eyes, she was surprised to see that several of the lamps were out. A number of chairs and couches were empty. She glanced at her watch: it was nearly ten. She must have drifted off. Across the room, the elderly couple was no longer there. She wanted to say good night to them, but they must have gone up to their room while her eyes were closed. She wished they would come back so that she could say good night to them.

Wearily Judith pushed herself to her feet. She would sleep well tonight.

In her room Judith changed quickly into her nightgown and set her alarm for twenty of six. In bed she picked up the book on Victorian architecture, but she could scarcely keep her eyes open. Her body was deliciously tired; there was no need to read herself to sleep. Turning out the lamp beside the bed, she closed her eyes and felt herself falling down, down, toward deepest sleep.

But something was wrong; she could not fall asleep. She turned from side to side, searching restlessly for sleep, as if it lay waiting for her in some precise portion of the bed. No doubt her nap—that disastrous little nap—had taken the edge off her tiredness. And yet she was tired, she longed for sleep. It was a mistake not to have read a little, as she always did. When she looked at the clock, she saw with dismay that it was eleven-thirty-five. Even if she fell asleep instantly she would get only six hours of sleep. It was hopeless. She felt doomed.

Judith turned on the bed lamp, grimly opened the book on Victorian architecture, and began to read. The sentences struck her as at once childish and pedantic, as if she were being lectured by a bright eighth-grader who had taken notes from a dubious encyclopedia. Instead of flowing from one to the next, the sentences stumbled against each other and walked off in every direction, rubbing their shins. The margins were comically wide. For the sake of the photographs the text had been printed on shiny stock, and the bedlamp glared on the print, which for that matter should have been two points larger. The stillness of the room, the whiteness and dryness of her fingers in the glow of the lamp, her blue leather suitcase standing stiffly on the rug, all these began to irritate her, to fill her with anger and unhappiness. Even the steady, monotonous beating of her heart exasperated her—she could feel it in there, drudging away, preventing sleep.

She slammed the book shut and sat up. It was nearly midnight. Oh, it was hopeless; she was making things worse by staying in bed. She needed to move about, to do something; and it came to her that she would return the book to the library.

Quickly she threw the covers off and changed into a sweater, jeans, and slippers.

Her eyelids were heavy but she felt restlessly awake as she walked swiftly along the dim-lit corridor past dark, slumbering doors. At the top of the main stairway she placed her hand on the smooth wood of the banister and hurried down the thick-carpeted stairs. At the bottom she saw light coming from the main lounge. Softly she walked over to the open doorway; she was surprised to see two elderly women reading quietly in armchairs. They did not look up, and Judith tiptoed away. She went back through the lobby, turned down a small corridor, and entered the Winter Lounge. A single lamp was lit; the lounge was deserted. The door of the library was open and a faint light streamed into the darkness of the lounge.

When Judith entered the library she did not at first see the dark woman. A single dim lamp was lit, on a little table beside an empty armchair with a flowered slipcover, and her gaze first fell on the lamplit pink flowers of the chair. The woman sat alone on a dark couch across from the lamp. She turned her head as Judith entered.

"I didn't know you'd be here," Judith said sharply. But of course the woman would be. She was everywhere.

"Were you looking for me?" the other asked.

"No," Judith said quietly, as if she were suppressing a shout. "I couldn't sleep. I came to return a book." She held up the book, as if to show that she wasn't lying. She entered the room quickly and began looking nervously about, peering at the dark rows of books, searching for the proper space.

"Almost no one comes in here. I hope you won't mind if I speak frankly. You see, I have feelings sometimes, deep within, and I trust what they tell me. This morning on the tower I felt so certain you wanted to speak to me."

"To speak to you?" Holding the book in both hands, as if it were as large as a storm window, Judith turned to look at her.

"Yes, to speak. To me. I felt so certain that was what you wanted."

Judith laughed lightly and, raising a hand in nervous irritation, smoothed back her dark hair. "I really think you— and you say you have these feelings?"

"Yes. I feel that you are so unhappy."

The words burst into flame within Judith. She could scarcely breathe.

"I see. Thank you very much."

"Please. There's no need to sound that way. To hold things inside. Won't you sit down?"

"I'm perfectly all right. Thank you. I came to return a book." She thrust it between two books as if she had stolen it. "There. Thank you. I am perfectly fine."

Judith turned and walked violently from the room.

She hurried up the stairway and along the dark corridor. Once she nearly stumbled, and gave a gasp that seemed as loud as a cry. In her room she locked the door and lay down on the bed. Her heart was beating savagely. Rage surged in her—the rudeness of that witch, the insolence. She was obviously insane. "You see, I have feelings sometimes, deep within." She had spoken gently, calmly; she was insane. "I feel you are so unhappy." How dare she feel anything at all? That demented woman had looked at her with pity. Judith sat up abruptly and walked over to the mirror on the door. In the dim lamplight her face looked pale and worn, her dark eyes mournful. She returned to the bed and lay down. Ah, how dare she? "I feel you are so unhappy." The sentimental words burned in her—she was burning up in them. Unhappiness like a fire broke out in her. Alone in her room, Judith wept. The tears shocked her; she couldn't stop. She wept because the woman had looked at her kindly and with pity. She wept because she was alone in a place where lovers lay on the rocks. She wept because things had not turned out the way she had hoped. She wept because she had loved the wrong man, she wept because she was no longer young, she wept because she had started and could not stop. She wept like a child, passionately, with terrible conviction. Her tears seemed to burn a flaming passage through her life. But it was intolerable. She detested it—the banality of tears. Grief wasn't a flame—it was riot, it was madness. It had sprung to life at a madwoman's touch. There was no reason for it. But it had fooled her; it must have been waiting there all along. She wept again for her beautiful weak man, who had done such terrible harm. She had been his greatest accomplice. With his hands in his pockets he had come strolling into her life, looking nervously about. He had not been sure, he had never been sure. And she, overflowing with new powers of sympathy, had beautifully understood. She had blossomed with understanding, she had grown brilliant with it. And so he had settled down uncertainly, looking at her with his beautiful nervous eyes, and she had dared to be happy: she had done that thing. And he had left, in stages; he had shown weakness even in that, while she in her panic had spun round him glittering delicate threads of understanding. Judith wept for those glittering threads, and for the fire that had raged in her, and for the deadness that had slowly come over things. She wept at the waste of it. She shook with weeping, it poured out of her, she couldn't stop.

As Judith wept, her unhappiness seemed to expand and grow more generous. She wept for the lovers on the sun-flooded cliff, who did not know what lay ahead. She wept for the elderly couple, who perhaps woke in the night, trembling with death fear. She wept for the dark woman, who in the arrogance of her sadness had developed cruel gifts of divination. Judith felt herself dilate with unhappiness; and as she wept, her sorrow grew rich and darkly lovely, a black flower, opening petal by velvet petal.

For a while it seemed as if she would sleep. But again it struck her, shaking her like an illness. She got up from the bed and walked weeping around the nearly dark room. She felt ugly with sorrow, as if her tears were wearing lines into her face. Damn the witch. She was too tired for this.

She lay down, exhausted, and it flashed in her that this would end. It was bound to end. Everything ended. Tomorrow she would be sitting in sunshine on her red bench. She would eat dinner early, take the limousine to the bus station, and ride toward the city in the dark. In the morning she would be at her desk. There were letters to dictate, a meeting at ten with the three new trainees, and a luncheon appointment with the author of a college math text that proposed to teach the concept of number by using the history of number systems in different cultures. She wouldn't have a minute to spare for sorrow, and if the thought of the tears now pouring from her came into her mind, they would seem as dreamlike and implausible as her father's explanation, when she was a child, that the lawn on which they were standing was part of a great globe that was not only turning round and round but was rushing along like a ball shot out of a cannon.

But it was ugly; humiliating. She was helpless against it. She lay on the bed, utterly given over to grief. Her grief seemed to be growing stronger, as if it were gaining confidence. It was not ennobling, it was not even interesting. People suffered the way they loved—not with their hearts but with their stomachs. It bored her. But still it went on.

And again it struck at her, the ugly and humiliating thing. It overmastered her, ranging through her at will. Judith lay weakly on her pillow and felt herself slowly give up. She tried to remember if she had ever felt peaceful, and it seemed to her that long ago, in some other life, she had sat in sunlight. She no longer existed; she was only a lump of ugly suffering.

She had no respect for these tears, these shakings. Weak, weak, she was weak. Weak! She despised weepy women.

The thought came to her that she might be having a breakdown. At the thought a terror came over her; calmed for a moment by terror, she forced herself up from the bed.

She walked over to the window and pushed aside the shade. She was startled to see her shocked face staring at her from the dark glass. Through her face she saw black hills and a dark-blue sky rich with stars. Once when she was a child her father had taken her out at night to the top of the driveway and let her look through his telescope at the moon and stars. The telescope stood on a tripod and he had lowered the legs for her. He had told her that a long time ago people believed the sky was a bowl filled with little holes, and that the stars were those little holes, through which the sun was shining. He had explained gravely and carefully what the stars really were, but she had come away knowing that the night was a bowl with the sun shining through the holes.

A coolness flowed from the glass. Judith leaned forward toward the coolness and saw her pale face bowing to meet her. She pressed her burning forehead against the cool glass. The room seemed stifling, unbearable. The whole room was filled with sorrow. All at once she released the shade; it clattered as if she had hurled it against the glass. She went over to the bed and began to put on her hiking boots.

Struggling to pull her arm through a sweater she stepped into the hall. Her head ached and tears burned in her eyes. At the top of the stairs she stopped to button her sweater; it was black with black buttons. She placed her hand on the smooth wood of the banister and watched the hand slide down alongside her as she swiftly descended. At the bottom the hand swept up over the wooden globe of the stairpost and joined her again. From the lobby she passed into the empty lounge, where a single lamp dimly glowed. An old woman was asleep in a chair. Judith stepped through the side door onto the dark veranda, hurried down the steps onto the gravel path, and stopped.

The moon shocked her: it was burning white. It had burned the blackness out of the sky, leaving a radiant dark blue. She felt like breaking off a piece of the moon and pressing it against her forehead, plunging it into her mouth. She felt crazed. Tears streamed along her face.

She had come out with no plan except to escape the sorrow in her room, but as if she knew where she wanted to go she did not hesitate. The moon would light her way.

The twisting downward path was speckled with pale patches of moonlight. A stone cast a sharp shadow. She could see leaf shadows printed on the path. Overhead the night was so deeply blue that she refused to believe it; she was reminded of the fraudulent and enchanting skies of night scenes in old Technicolor movies. A nearby crackle startled her. She had read that there were possums, raccoons, and deer in the woods. Judith had never seen a possum. What if one leaped out at her? She wouldn't even know what it was.

When she reached the bench at the bend of the path she stopped in surprise. It had no color, though the moon shone on part of it—it was only darkness and light. There, where she had been peaceful, she sat down.

On the brilliantly moonlit cliff the gazebo cast a hard-edged shadow. There were many parallel stripes and criss-crosses. Through the pale, radiant beams of the gazebo she could see diamonds and parallelograms of dark-blue night. Near the pointed roof-shadow something gleamed, and she recognized the beer can. It threw a long shadow. At the very edge of the cliff, brightness turned into darkness. She tried to see the precise place where the brightness stopped.

She raised a hand to her face and was startled to feel wetness there. She remembered that she had been crying. The woman had hurt her. And at the memory it began again: something rose in her and she was shaken with it, she wept and bent her face into her hands. She took deep breaths, as if she had to reach far down to find strength for her sorrow. Her body shook, her ribs ached, her shoulders hunched old-womanishly.

She could not stop. She wept as if some deep restraint of pride or breeding had given way in her. She wept beyond shame, crudely and obscenely, as if grief were a form of ugliness she could no longer escape. She had no sympathy for the grief that filled her and shook her, that seemed too large for her, as if it did not fit her insides correctly. Her grief was the wrong size. It spilled out of her and left her far behind. It was larger than the Mountain Lodge, larger than anything; and it seemed to her that she had left her room and come out into the night because only the night was large enough.

Sick with sorrow, twisted with grief, Judith stumbled from the bench and struck for the path leading to the cliff. She wanted to run away from her unhappiness, to leave it behind. Trembling and weeping she emerged from the trees into a brilliance of moonlight. The moon hurt her tear-burned eyes. Now that she was out of the woods Judith advanced slowly, as if her hair had become tangled in the brilliance of the night sky—in twigs and branches of light. The moonlight tore at her hair. The blazing beer can stunned her, distracted her. She looked up at the moon. It burned out her eyes. She came to the edge of the cliff, where the dark place began.

She looked down, and the dark seemed to reach up and seize her ankles. A dizziness came over her. She felt herself falling into the soothing dark. Her hair streamed in the wind of her falling; and as she fell down and down, she felt her sorrow streaming from her like a wind. It was blowing out of her in all directions. It was spreading through the dark hills and valleys, flowing into the night sky, rising higher and higher, slowly filling the blue bowl of night.

Judith opened her eyes. She looked about. She stepped back suddenly. She was standing near the edge of a cliff. She

A Day in the Country

looked at the edge of the cliff. She looked up at the moon. It was night. There was a moon in the sky.

Judith raised a hand and smoothed back her hair. She said: "My name is Judith Hahn. This is a rock. That is the moon. Shhh. It's all right. Shhh. It's over now. You can go back. Shhh, dear. That's all right. Go back. Shhh."

Obediently, Judith turned and went slowly back up the path.

III

Snowmen

One sunny morning I woke and pushed aside a corner of the blinds. Above the frosted, sun-dazzled bottom of the glass I saw a brilliant blue sky, divided into luminous rectangles by the orderly white strips of wood in my window. Down below, the back yard had vanished. In its place was a dazzling white sea, whose lifted and immobile waves would surely have toppled if I had not looked at them just then. It had happened secretly, in the night. It had snowed with such abandon, such fervor, such furious delight, that I could not understand how that wildness of snowing had failed to wake me with its white roar. The topmost twigs of the tall back-yard hedge poked through the whiteness, but here and there a great drift covered them. The silver chains of the bright-yellow swing-frame plunged into snow. Snow rose high above the floor of the old chicken coop at the back of the garage, and snow on the chicken-coop roof swept up to the top of the garage gable. In the corner of the white yard the tilted clothespole rose out of the snow like the mast of a sinking ship. A reckless snow-wave, having dashed against the side of the pole, flung up a line of frozen spray, as if straining to pull it all under. From the flat roof of the chicken coop hung a row of thick icicles, some in sun and some in shade. They reminded me of glossy and matte prints in my father's albums. Under the sunny icicles were dark holes in the snow where the water dripped. Suddenly I remembered a rusty

rake-head lying teeth down in the dirt of the vegetable garden. It seemed more completely buried than ships under the
sea, or the quartz and flint arrowheads that were said to lie
under the dark loam of the garden, too far down for me to
ever find them, forever out of reach.

I hurried downstairs, shocked to discover that I was expected to eat breakfast on such a morning. In the sunny
yellow kitchen I dreamed of dark tunnels in the snow. There
was no exit from the house that day except by way of the
front door. A thin, dark, wetly gleaming trail led between
high snowbanks to the two cement steps before the buried
sidewalk, where it stopped abruptly, as if in sudden discour-
agement. Jagged hills of snow thrown up by the snowplow
rose higher than my head. I climbed over the broken slabs
and reached the freedom of the street. Joey Czukowski and
Mario Salvio were already there. They seemed struck with
wonder. Earmuffs up and cap-peaks pulled low, they both
held snowballs in their hands, as if they did not know what
to do with them. Together we roamed the neighborhood in
search of Jimmy Shaw. Here and there great gaps appeared
in the snow-ranges, revealing a plowed driveway and a vista
of snowy yard. At the side of Mario's house a sparkling drift
swept up to the windowsill. A patch of bright-green grass, in
a valley between drifts, startled us as if waves had parted and
we were looking at the bottom of the sea. High above, white
and black against the summer-blue sky, the telephone wires
were heaped with snow. Heavy snow-lumps fell thudding. We
found Jimmy Shaw banging a stick against a snow-covered
STOP sign on Collins Street. Pagliaro's lot disturbed us: in
summer we fought there with ashcan covers, sticks, and rusty
cans, and now its dips and rises, its ripples and contours,
which we knew as intimately as we knew our cellar floors, had
been transformed into a mysterious new pattern of humps
and hollows, an unknown realm reminding us of the vanished
lot only by the distorted swelling of its central hill.

Dizzy with discovery, we spent that morning wandering the newly invented streets of more alien neighborhoods. From a roof gutter hung a glistening four-foot icicle, thick as a leg. Now and then we made snowballs, and feebly threw ourselves into the conventional postures of a snowball fight, but our hearts were not really in it—they had surrendered utterly to the inventions of the snow. There was about our snow a lavishness, an ardor, that made us restless, exhilarated, and a little uneasy, as if we had somehow failed to measure up to that white extravagance.

It was not until the afternoon that the first snowmen appeared. There may have been some in the morning, but I did not see them, or perhaps they were only the usual kind and remained lost among the enchantments of the snow. But that afternoon we began to notice them, in the shallower places of front and back yards. And we accepted them at once, indeed were soothed by them, as if only they could have been the offspring of such snow. They were not commonplace snowmen composed of three big snowballs piled one on top of the other, with carrots for noses and big black buttons or smooth round stones for eyes. No, they were passionately detailed men and women and children of snow, with noses and mouths and chins of snow. They wore hats of snow and coats of snow. Their shoes of snow were tied with snow-laces. One snowgirl in a summer dress of snow and a straw hat of snow stood holding a delicate snow-parasol over one shoulder.

I imagined that some child in the neighborhood, made restless by our snow, had fashioned the first of these snow statues, perhaps little more than an ordinary snowman with roughly sculpted features. Once seen, the snowman had been swiftly imitated in one yard after another, always with some improvement—and in that rivalry that passes from yard to yard, new intensities of effort had led to finer and finer figures. But perhaps I was mistaken. Perhaps the truth was that a child of genius, maddened and inspired by our fervent snow, had in a burst of rapture created a new kind of snowman, perfect in every detail, which others later copied with varied success.

Fevered and summoned by those snowmen, we returned to our separate yards. I made my snowman in a hollow between the swing and the crab-apple tree. My first efforts were clumsy and oppressive, but I restrained my impatience and soon felt a passionate discipline come over me. My hands were inspired, it was as if I were coaxing into shape a form that longed to spring forth from the fecund snow. I shaped the eyelids, gave a tenseness to the narrow nostrils, completed the tight yet faintly smiling lips, and stepped back to admire my work. Beyond the chicken coop, in Joey's yard, I saw him admiring his own. He had made an old woman in a babushka, carrying a basket of eggs.

Together we went to Mario's yard, where we found him furiously completing the eyes of a caped and mustached magician who held in one hand a hollow top hat of snow from which he was removing a long-eared rabbit. We applauded him enviously and all three went off to find Jimmy Shaw, who had fashioned two small girls holding hands. I secretly judged his effort sentimental, yet was impressed by his leap into doubleness.

Restless and unappeased, we set out again through the neighborhood, where already a change was evident. The stiffly standing snowmen we had seen earlier in the afternoon were giving way to snowmen that assumed a variety of poses. One, with head bent and a hand pressed to his hat, appeared to be walking into a wind, which blew back the skirt of his long coat. Another, in full stride, had turned with a frown to look over his shoulder, and you could see the creases in his jacket of snow. A third bowed low from the waist, his hat swept out behind him. We returned dissatisfied to our yards. My snowman looked dull, stiff, and vague. I threw myself into the fashioning of a more lively snowman, and as the sun sank below a rooftop I stood back to admire my snowy father, sitting in an armchair of snow with one leg hooked over the arm, holding a book in one hand as, with the other, he turned a single curling page of snow.

Yet even then I realized that it was not enough, that already it had been surpassed, that new forms yearned to be born from our restless, impetuous snow.

That night I could scarcely sleep. With throbbing temples and burning eyes I hurried through breakfast and rushed outside. It was just as I had suspected: a change had been wrought. I could feel it everywhere. Perhaps bands of feverish children, tormented by white dreams, had worked secretly through the night.

The snowmen had grown more marvelous. Groups of snowy figures were everywhere. In one back yard I saw three ice skaters of snow, their heels lifted and their scarves of snow streaming out behind them. In another yard I saw, gripping their instruments deftly, the fiercely playing members of a string quartet. Individual figures had grown more audacious. On a back-yard clothesline I saw a snowy tightrope walker with a long balancing stick of snow, and in another yard I saw a juggler holding two snowballs in one hand while, suspended in the air, directly above his upward-gazing face. . . . But it was precisely a feature of that second day, when the art of the snowman appeared to reach a fullness, that one could no longer be certain to what extent the act of seeing had itself become infected by these fiery snow-dreams. And just when it seemed that nothing further could be dreamed, the snow animals began to appear. I saw a snow lion, a snow elephant with uplifted trunk, a snow horse rearing, a snow gazelle. But once the idea of "snowman," already fertile with instances, had blossomed to include animals, new and dizzying possibilities presented themselves, for there was suddenly nothing to prevent further sproutings and germinations; and it was then that I began to notice, among the graceful white figures and the daring, exquisite animals, the first maples and willows of snow.

It was on the afternoon of that second day that the passion for replication reached heights none of us could have foreseen. Sick with ecstasy, pained with wonder, I walked the white streets with Joey Czukowski and Mario Salvio and Jimmy Shaw. "Look at that!" one of us would cry, and "Cripes, look at that!" Our own efforts had already been left far behind, but it no longer mattered, for the town itself had been struck with genius. Trees of snow had been composed leaf by leaf, with visible veins, and upon the intricate twigs and branches of snow, among the white foliage, one could see white sparrows, white cardinals, white jays. In one yard we saw a garden of snow tulips, row on row. In another yard we saw a snow fountain with arching water jets of finespun snow. And in one back yard we saw an entire parlor all of snow, with snow lamps and snow tables and, in a snow fireplace, logs and flames of snow. Perhaps it was this display that inspired one of the more remarkable creations of that afternoon—in the field down by the stream, dozens of furiously intense children were completing a great house of snow, with turrets and gables and chimneys of snow, and splendid rooms of snow, with floors of snow and furniture of snow, and stairways of snow and mirrors of snow, and cups and rafters and sugar bowls of snow, and, on a mantelpiece of marble snow, a clock of snow with a moving ice pendulum.

I think it was the very thoroughness of these successes that produced in me the first stirrings of uneasiness, for I sensed in our extravagant triumphs an inner impatience. Already, it seemed to me, our snowmen were showing evidence of a skill so excessive, an elaboration so painfully and exquisitely minute, that it could scarcely conceal a desperate restlessness. Someone had fashioned a leafy hedge of snow in which he had devised an intricate snow spiderweb, whose frail threads shimmered in the late afternoon light. Someone else had fashioned a kaleidoscope of snow, which turned to reveal, in delicate ice mirrors, changing arabesques of snow. And on the far side of town we discovered an entire park of snow, already abandoned by its makers: the pine trees had pine-cones of snow and individual snow needles, on the snow picnic tables lay fallen acorns of snow, snow burrs caught on our trouser legs, and under an abandoned swing of snow I found, beside an empty Coke bottle made of snow, a snow nickel with a perfectly rendered buffalo.

Exhausted by these prodigies, I sought to pierce the out-ward shapes and seize the unquiet essence of the snow, but I saw only whiteness there. That night I spent in anxious dreams, and I woke feverish and unrefreshed to a sunny morning.

The world was still white, but snow was dripping every-where. Icicles, longer and more lovely, shone forth in a last, desperate brilliance, rainspouts trickled, rills of bright black snow-water rushed along the sides of streets and poured through the sewer grates. I did not notice them at first, the harbingers of the new order. It was Mario who pointed the first one out to me. From the corner of a roof it thrust out over the rainspout. I did not understand it, but I was filled with happiness. I began to see others. They projected from roof corners, high above the yards, their smiles twisted in mockery. These gargoyles of snow had perhaps been shaped as a whim, a joke, a piece of childish exuberance, but as they spread through the town I began to sense their true meaning. They were nothing less than a protest against the solemnity, the rigidity, of our snowmen. What had seemed a blossoming forth of hidden powers, that second afternoon, suddenly seemed a form of intricate constriction. It was as if those bird-filled maples, those lions, those leaping ballerinas and pranc-ing clowns had been nothing but a failure of imagination.

On that third and last day, when our snowmen, weary with consummation, swerved restlessly away, I sensed a fever in the wintry air, as if everyone knew that such strains and ec-stasies were bound to end quickly. Scarcely had the gargoyles sprouted from the roofs when, among the trees and tigers, one began to see trolls and ogres and elves. They squatted in

the branches of real elms and snow elms, they peeked out
through the crossed slats of porch aprons, they hid behind
the skirts of snow women. Fantastical snowbirds appeared,
nobly lifting their white, impossible wings. Griffins, unicorns,
and sea serpents enjoyed a brief reign before being surpassed
by splendid new creatures that disturbed us like half-forgot-
ten dreams. Here and there rose fanciful dwellings, like
feverish castles, like fairy palaces glimpsed at the bottoms of
lakes on vanished summer afternoons, with soaring pinnacles,
twisting passageways, stairways leading nowhere, snow chambers seen in fever-dreams.

Yet even these visions of the morning partook of the very
world they longed to supplant, and it was not until the afternoon that our snowmen began to achieve freedoms so
dangerous that they threatened to burn out the eyes of be-
holders. It was then that distorted, elongated, disturbingly
supple figures began to replace our punctilious imitations.
And yet I sensed that they were not distortions, those un-
graspable figures, but direct expressions of shadowy inner
realms. To behold them was to be filled with a sharp, troubled
joy. As the afternoon advanced, and the too-soon-darkening
sky warned us of transitory pleasures, I felt a last, intense
straining. My nerves trembled, my ears rang with white music.
A new mystery was visible everywhere. It was as if snow were
throwing off the accident of accumulated heaviness and returning to its original airiness. Indeed these spiritual forms,
disdaining the earth, seemed scarcely to be composed of white
substance, as if they were striving to escape from the limits
of snow itself. Walking the ringing streets in the last light, my
nerves stretched taut, I felt in that last rapture of snow a lofty
and criminal striving, and all my senses seemed to dissolve in
the dark pleasures of transgression.

Drained by these difficult joys, I was not unhappy when
the rain came.

It rained all that night, and far into the morning. In the
afternoon the sun came out. Bright-green grass shone among

thin patches of snow. Joey Czukowski, Mario Salvio, Jimmy Shaw, and I roamed the neighborhood before returning to my cellar for a game of ping-pong. Brilliant black puddles shone in the sunny streets. Here and there on snow-patched lawns we saw remains of snowmen, but so melted and disfigured that they were only great lumps of snow. We did not discuss the events of the last few days, which already seemed as fantastic as vanished icicles, as unseizable as fading dreams. "Look at that!" cried Mario, and pointed up. On a telephone wire black as licorice, stretched against the bright blue sky, a bluejay sat and squawked. Suddenly it flew away. A dark-yellow willow burned in the sun. On a wooden porch step I saw a brilliant red bowl. "Let's do something," said Joey, and we tramped back to my house, our boots scraping against the asphalt, our boot buckles jangling.

In the Penny Arcade

In the summer of my twelfth birthday I stepped from August sunshine into the shadows of the penny arcade. My
father and mother had agreed to wait outside, on a green
bench beside the brilliant white ticket booth. Even as I entered
the shade cast by the narrow overhang, I imagined my mother
gazing anxiously after me from under her wide-brimmed
summer hat, as if she might lose me forever in that intricate
darkness, while my father, supporting the sun-polished bowl
of his pipe with one hand, and frowning as if angrily in the
intense light, for he refused to wear either a hat or sunglasses,
had already begun studying the signs on the dart-and-balloon
booth and the cotton-candy stand, in order to demonstrate to
me that he was not overly anxious on my account. After all,
I was a big boy now. I had not been to the amusement park
for two years. I had dreamed of it all that tense, enigmatic
summer, when the world seemed hushed and expectant, as if
on the verge of revealing an overwhelming secret. Inside the
penny arcade I saw at once that the darkness was not dark
enough. I had remembered a plunge into the enticing darkness of movie theaters on hot bright summer afternoons, but
here sunlight entered through the open doorway shaded by
the narrow overhanging roof. Through a high window a shaft
of sunlight fell, looking as if it had been painted with a wide
brush onto the dusty air. Among the mysterious ringing of
bells, the clanks, the metallic whirrings of the penny arcade I

could hear the bright, prancing, secretly mournful music of the merry-go-round and the cries and clatter of the distant roller coaster.

The darkness seemed thicker toward the back of the penny arcade, as if it had retreated from the open doorway and gathered more densely there. Slowly I made my way deeper in. Tough teenagers with hair slicked back on both sides stood huddled over the pinball machines. In their dangerous hair, rich with violence, I could see the deep lines made by their combs, like knife cuts in wood. I passed a glass case containing a yellow toy derrick sitting on a heap of prizes: plastic rings, flashlight pens, little games with holes and silver balls, black rubber tarantulas, red-hots and licorice pipes. Before the derrick a father held up a little blond girl in red shorts and a blue T-shirt; working the handle, she tried to make the jaws of the derrick close over a prize, which kept slipping back into the pile. Nearby, a small boy sat gripping a big black wheel that controlled a car racing on a screen. A tall muscular teenager with a blond crewcut and sullen gray eyes stood bent over a pinball machine that showed luminous Hawaiian girls with red flowers in their gleaming black hair; each time his finger pushed the button, a muscle tensed visibly in his dark, bare upper arm. For a moment I was tempted by the derrick, but at once despised my childishness and continued on my way. It was not prizes I had come out of the sun for. It was something else I had come for, something mysterious and elusive that I could scarcely name. Tense with longing, with suppressed excitement, and with the effort of appearing tough, dangerous, and inconspicuous, I came at last to the old fortune teller in her glass booth.

Through the dusty glass I saw that she had aged. Her red turban was streaked with dust, one of her pale blue eyes had nearly faded away, and her long, pointing finger, suspended above a row of five dusty and slightly upcurled playing cards, was chipped at the knuckle. A crack showed in the side of her nose. Her one good eye had a vague and vacant look, as if she had misplaced something and could no longer remember what it was. She looked as if the long boredom of uninterrupted meditation had withered her spirit. A decayed spiderweb stretched between her sleeve and wrist.

I remembered how I had once been afraid of looking into her eyes, unwilling to be caught in that deep, mystical gaze. Feeling betrayed and uneasy, I abandoned her and went off in search of richer adventures.

The merry-go-round music had stopped, and far away I heard the cry: "Three tries for two bits! Everybody a winner!" I longed to escape from these sounds, into the lost beauty and darkness of the penny arcade. I passed several dead-looking games and rounded the corner of a big machine that printed your name on a disk of metal. I found him standing against the wall, beside a dusty pinball machine with a piece of tape over its coin-slot. No one seemed to be paying attention to him. He was wearing a black cowboy hat pulled low over his forehead, a black shirt, wrinkled black pants, and black, cracked boots with nickel-colored spurs. He had long black sideburns and a thin black mustache. His black belt was studded with white wooden bullets. In the center of his chest was a small red target. He stood with one arm held away from his side, the hand gripping a black pistol that pointed down. Facing him stood a post to which was attached a holster with a gun. From the butt of the gun came a coiled black rubber wire that ran into the post. A faded sign gave directions in tiny print. I slid the holster to hip level and, stepping up against it, practiced my draw. Then I placed a dime carefully in the shallow depression of the coin-slot, pushed the metal tongue in and out, and grasped the gun. I heard a whirring sound. Suddenly someone began to speak; I looked quickly about, but the voice came from the cowboy's stomach. I had forgotten. Slowly, wearily, as if dragging their way reluctantly up from a deep well, the words struggled forth. "All . . . right . . . you . . . dirty . . . side . . . winder. . . . Drrrrraw!" I drew my gun and shot him in the heart. The cowboy stood dully staring at me, as if he were wondering without interest why I had just killed him. Then slowly, slowly, he began to raise his gun. I could feel the strain of that slow raising in my own tensed arm. When the gun was pointing a little to the left of my stomach, he stopped. I heard a dim, soft bang. Wearily, as if from far away, he said: "Take . . . that . . . you . . . low . . . down . . . varmint." Slowly he began to lower his burdensome gun. When the barrel was pointing downward, I heard the whirring stop. I looked about; a little girl holding a candied apple in a fat fist stared up at me without expression. In rage and sorrow I strode away.

I passed the little men with boxing gloves standing stiffly in their glass case, but I knew better than to try to stir them into sluggish and inept life. A desolation had fallen over the creatures of the penny arcade. Even the real, live people strolling noisily about had become infected with the general woodenness; their laughter sounded forced, their gestures seemed exaggerated and unconvincing. I felt caught in an atmosphere of decay and disappointment. I felt that if I could not find whatever it was I was looking for, my entire life would be harmed. Making my way along narrow aisles flanked by high, clattering games, I turned left and right among them, scorning their unmysterious pleasures, until at last I came to a section of old machines, in a dusky recess near the back of the hall.

The machines stood close together, as if huddling in dark, disreputable comradeship, yet with a careless and indifferent air among them. Three older boys, one of whom had a pack of cigarettes tucked into the rolled-up sleeve of his T-shirt, stood peering into three viewers. I chose a machine as far from them as possible. A faded picture in dim colors showed a woman with faded yellow hair standing with her back to me and looking over her shoulder with a smile. She was wearing a tall white hat that had turned nearly gray, a faded white tuxedo jacket, faded black nylon stockings with a black line up the back, and faded red high-heels. In one hand she held a cane with which she reached behind her, lifting slightly the back of her jacket to reveal the tense top of one stocking and the bottom of a faded garter. With a feeling of oppression I placed my dime in the slot and leaned my face onto the metal viewer. Its edges pressed against the bones of my face as if it had seized me and pulled me close. I pushed the metal tongue in and out; for a moment nothing happened. Then a title appeared: A DAY AT THE CIRCUS. It vanished to reveal a dim woman in black-and-white who was standing on a horse in an outdoor ring surrounded by well-dressed men and women. She was wearing a tight costume with a little skirt and did not look like the woman in the picture. As the horse trotted slowly round and round the ring, sometimes leaping jerkily forward as the film jerkily unreeled, she stood on one leg and reached out the other leg behind her. Once she jumped in the air and landed looking the other way, and once she stood on her hands. The men and women strained to see past each other's shoulders; sometimes they looked at each other and nodded vigorously. I waited for something to happen, for some un-spoken promise to be fulfilled, but all at once the movie ended. Desperately dissatisfied I tried to recall the troubling, half-naked woman I had seen two years earlier, but my mem-ory was vague and uncertain; perhaps I had not even dared to peer into the forbidden viewer.

I left the machines and began walking restlessly through the loud hall, savoring its shame, its fall from mystery. It seemed to me that I must have walked into the wrong arcade; I wondered whether there was another one in a different part of the amusement park, the true penny arcade that had en-chanted my childhood. It seemed as though a blight had overtaken the creatures of this hall: they were sickly, wasted versions of themselves. Perhaps they were impostors, who had treacherously overthrown the true creatures and taken their place. Anxiously I continued my sad wandering, searching for something I could no longer understand—a nuance, a mys-tery, a dark glimmer. Under a pinball machine I saw a cone of paper covered with sticky pink wisps. An older boy in jeans and a white T-shirt, wearing a dark-green canvas apron divided into pockets bulging with coins, looked sharply about for customers who needed change. I came to a shadowy region at the back of the hall; there was no one about. I noticed that the merry-go-round music had stopped again. The machines in this region had an old and melancholy look. I passed them without interest, turned a corner, and saw before me a dark alcove.

A thick rope of blue velvet, attached to two posts, stretched in a curve before the opening. In the darkness within I saw a jumble of dim shapes, some covered with cloths like furniture in a closed room in a decaying mansion in a movie. I felt something swell within me, as if my temples would burst; at the same time I was extraordinarily calm. I knew that these must be the true machines and creatures of the penny arcade, and that for some unaccountable reason they had been removed to make way for the sad impostors whose shameful performance I had witnessed. I looked quickly behind me; I could barely breathe. With a feeling that at any moment I might dissolve, I stepped over the rope and entered the forbidden dark.

It was too dark for me to see clearly, but some other sense was so heightened that I was almost painfully alert. I could feel the mystery of these banished machines, their promise of rich and intricate excitements. I could not understand why they had been set apart in this enchanted cavern, but I had no doubt that here was the lost penny arcade, crowded with all that I had longed for and almost forgotten. With fearful steps I came to a machine carelessly covered with a cloth; peering intensely at the exposed portion, I caught a glimpse of cracked glass. At that moment I heard a sound behind me, and in terror I whirled around.

No one was there. A hush had fallen over the penny arcade. I hurried to the rope and stepped into safety. At first I thought the hall had become strangely deserted, but I saw several people walking slowly and quietly about. It appeared that one of those accidental hushes had fallen over things, as sometimes happens in a crowd: the excitement dies down, for an instant the interwoven cries and voices become unraveled, quietness pours into the suddenly open spaces from which it had been excluded. In that hush, anything might happen. All my senses had burst wide open. I was so tense with inner excitement, which pressed against my temples, that it seemed as if I would expand to fill the entire hall.

Through an intervening maze of machines I could see the black hat brim and black elbow of the distant cowboy. In the tremulous stillness, which at any moment might dissolve, he seemed to await me.

Even as I approached I sensed that he had changed. He seemed more sure of himself, and he looked directly at me. His mouth wore an expression of faint mockery. I could feel his whole nature expanding and unfolding within him. From the shadow of his hat brim his eyes blazed darkly; for a moment I had the sensation of someone behind me. I turned, and saw in the glass booth across the hall the fortune teller staring at me with piercing blue eyes. Between her and the cowboy I could feel a dark complicity. Somewhere I heard a gentle creaking, and I became aware of small, subtle motions all about me. The creatures of the penny arcade were waking from their wooden torpor. At first I could not see an actual motion, but I realized that the position of the little boxers had changed slightly, that the fortune teller had raised a warning finger. Secret signals were passing back and forth. I heard another sound, and saw a little hockey player seated at the side of his painted wooden field. I turned back to the cowboy; he looked at me with ferocity and contempt. His black eyes blazed. I could see one of his hands quiver with alertness. A muscle in his cheek tensed. My temples were throbbing, I could scarcely breathe. I sensed that at any moment something forbidden was going to happen. I looked at his gun, which was now in his holster. I raised my eyes; he was ready.

As if mesmerized I put a dime in the slot and pushed the tongue in and out. For a moment he stared at me in cool fury. All at once he drew and fired—with such grace and swiftness, such deeply soothing swiftness, that something relaxed far back in my mind. I drew and fired, wondering whether I was already dead. He stood still, gazing at me with sudden calm. Grasping his stomach with both hands, he staggered slowly back, looking at me with an expression of flawless and magnificent malice. Gracefully he slumped to one knee, and bowed his unforgiving head as if in prayer; and falling slowly onto his side, he rolled onto his back with his arms outspread.

At once he rose, slapped dust from his pants, and returned to his original position. Radiant with spite, noble with venomous rancor, he looked at me with fierce amusement; I felt he was mocking me in some inevitable way. I knew that I hadn't a moment to lose, that I must seize my chance before it was too late. Tearing my eyes from his, I left him there in the full splendor of his malevolence.

Through the quiet hall I rushed furiously along. I came to a dusky recess near the back; no one was there. Thrusting in my dime, I pressed my hot forehead onto the cool metal. It was just as I thought: the woman slipped gracefully from her horse and, curtseying to silent applause, made her way through the crowd. She entered a dim room containing a bed with a carved mahogany headboard, and a tall swivel mirror suspended on a frame. She smiled at herself in the mirror, as if acknowledging that at last she had entered into her real existence. With a sudden rapid movement she began removing her costume. Beneath her disguise she was wearing a long jacket and a pair of black nylon stockings. Turning her back to the mirror and smiling over her shoulder, she lifted her jacket with the hook of her cane to reveal the top of her taut, dazzling stocking and a glittering garter. Teasingly she lifted it a little higher, then suddenly threw away the cane and began to unbutton her jacket. She frowned down and fumbled with the thick, clumsy buttons as I watched with tense impatience;

as the jacket came undone I saw something dim and shadowy beneath. At last she slipped out of the jacket, revealing a shimmering white slip which came to her knees. Quickly pulling the slip over her head, so that her face was concealed for a moment, she revealed a flowery blouse above a gleaming black girdle. Gripping the top of the girdle she began to peel it down, but it clung to her so tightly that she had to keep shifting her weight from leg to leg, her face grew dark, suddenly the girdle slipped off and revealed yet another tight and glimmering garment beneath, faster and faster she struggled out of her underwear, tossing each piece aside and revealing new and unsuspected depths of silken concealment, and always I had the sense that I was coming closer and closer to a dark mystery that cunningly eluded me. Prodigal and exuberant in her undressing, she offered a rich revelation of half-glimpses, an abundance of veiled and dusky disclosures. She blossomed with shimmer, silk, and shadow, ushering me into a lush and intricate realm of always more dangerous exposures which themselves proved to be new and dazzling concealments. Exhausted by these intensities, I watched her anxiously yet with growing languor, as if something vital in the pit of my stomach were being drawn forth and spun into the shimmer of her inexhaustible disrobings. She herself was lost in a feverish ecstasy, in the midst of which I detected a sadness, as if with each gesture she were grandly discarding parts of her life. I felt a melting languor, a feverish melancholy, until I knew that at any moment—"Hey!" I tore my face away. A boy in a yellow T-shirt was shouting at his friend. People strolled about, bells rang, children shouted in the penny arcade. Bright, prancing, sorrowful music from the merry-go-round turned round and round in the air. With throbbing temples I walked into the more open part of the arcade. The cowboy stood frozen in place, four boys in high-school jackets stood turning the rods from which the little hockey players hung down. Two small boys stood over the little boxers, who jerkily performed their motions. I turned around: in the dark alcove, before which stretched a blue velvet rope, I saw a collection of old, broken pinball machines. Across the hall the faded fortune teller sat dully in her dusty glass cage. A weariness had settled over the penny arcade. I felt tired and old, as if nothing could ever happen here. The strange hush, the waking of the creatures from their wooden slumber, seemed dim and uncertain, as if it had taken place long ago.

It was time to leave. Sadly I walked over to the wooden cowboy in his dusty black hat. I looked at him without forgiveness, taking careful note of the paint peeling from his hands. A boy of about my age stood before him, ready to draw. When the wooden figure began to speak, the boy burst into loud, mocking laughter. I felt the pain of that laughter burning in my chest, and I glanced reproachfully at the cowboy; from under the shadow of his hat his dull eyes seemed to acknowledge me. Slowly, jerkily, he began to raise his wooden arm. The lifting caused his head to shift slightly, and for an instant he cast at me a knowing gaze. An inner excitement seized me. Giving him a secret salute, I began walking rapidly about, as if stillness could not contain such illuminations.

All at once I had understood the secret of the penny arcade.

I understood with the force of an inner blow that the creatures of the penny arcade had lost their freedom under the constricting gaze of all those who no longer believed in them. Their majesty and mystery had been crushed down by the shrewd, oppressive eyes of countless visitors who looked at them without seeing their fertile inner nature. Gradually worn down into a parody of themselves, restricted to three or four preposterous wooden gestures, they yet contained within themselves the life that had once been theirs. Under the nourishing gaze of one who understood them, they might still spring into a semblance of their former selves. During the strange hush that had fallen over the arcade, the creatures had been freed from the paralyzing beams of commonplace attention that held them down as surely as the little ropes held down Gulliver in my illustrated book. I recognized that I myself had become part of the conspiracy of dullness, and that only in a moment of lavish awareness, which had left me confused and exhausted, had I seen truly. They had not betrayed me: I had betrayed them. I saw that I was in danger of becoming ordinary, and I understood that from now on I would have to be vigilant.

For this was the only penny arcade, the true penny arcade. There was no other.

Turning decisively, I walked toward the entrance and stepped into the dazzle of a perfect August afternoon. My mother and father shimmered on their bench, as if they were dissolving into light. In the glittering sandy dust beside their bench I saw the blazing white top of an ice-cream cup. My father was looking at his watch, my mother's face was turning toward me with a sorrowful expression that had already begun to change to deepest joy. A smell of saltwater from the beach beyond the park mingled with a smell of asphalt and cotton candy. Over the roof of the dart-and-balloon booth, silver airplanes were sailing lazily round and round at the ends of black cables in the brilliant blue sky. Shaking my head as if to clear it of shadows, I prepared myself to greet the simple pleasures of the sun.

Cathay

SINGING BIRDS

The twelve singing birds in the throne room of the Imperial Palace are made of beaten gold, except for the throats, which are of silver, and the eyes, which are of transparent emerald-green jade. The leaves of the great tree in which they sit are of copper, and the trunk and branches of opaque jade, the whole painted to imitate the natural colors of leaf, stem, and bark. When they sit on the branches, among the thick foliage, the birds are visible as only a glint of gold or flash of jade, although their sublime song is readily heard from every quarter of the throne room, and even in the outer hall. The birds do not always remain in the leaves, but now and then rise from their branches and fly about the tree. Sometimes one settles on the shoulder of the Emperor and pours into his ear the notes of its melodious and melancholy song. It is known that the tones are produced by an inner mechanism containing a minute crystalline pin, but the secret of its construction remains well guarded. The series of motions performed by the mechanical birds is of necessity repetitive, but the art is so skillful that one is never aware of recurrence, and indeed only by concentrating one's attention ruthlessly upon the motions of a single bird is one able, after a time, to discover at what point the series begins again, for the motions of all twelve birds are different and have been cleverly devised to draw attention away from any one of them. The shape and motions of the birds are so lifelike that they might easily be mistaken for real birds were it not for their golden forms, and many believe that it was to avoid such a mistake, and to increase our wonder, that the birds were permitted in this manner alone to retain the appearance of artifice.

CLOUDS

The clouds of Cathay are of an unusual purity of whiteness, and distinguish themselves clearly against the rich lapis lazuli of our skies. Perhaps for this reason we have been able to classify our cloud-shapes with a precision and thoroughness unknown to other lands. It may safely be said that no cloud in our heavens can assume a shape which has not already been named. The name is always of an object, natural or artificial, that exists in our empire, which is so vast that it is said to contain all things. Thus a cloud may be Wave Number One, or Wave Number Six Hundred Sixty-two, or Dragon's Tail Number Seven, or Wind in Wheat Number Forty-five, or Imperial Saddle Number Twenty-three. The result of our completeness is that our clouds lack the vagueness and indecision that sadden other skies, and are forbidden randomness except in the order of appearance of images. It is as if they are a fluid form of sculpture, arranging themselves at will into a succession of imitations. The artistry of our skies, for one well trained in the catalogues of shape, does not cause monotony by banishing the unknown; rather, it fills us with joyful surprise, as if, tossing into the air a handful of sand, one should see it assume, in quick succession, the shape of dragon, hourglass, stirrup, palace, swan.

THE CORRIDORS OF INSOMNIA

When the Emperor cannot sleep, he leaves his chamber and walks in either of two private corridors, which have been designed for this purpose and have become known as the Corridors of Insomnia. The corridors are so long that a man galloping on horseback would fail to reach the end of either in the space of a night. One corridor has walls of jade polished to the brightness of mirrors. The floor is covered with a scarlet carpet and the corridor is brightly lit by the fires of many chandeliers. In the jade mirrors, divided by vertical bands of gold, the Emperor can see himself endlessly reflected in depth after depth of dark green, while in the distance the perfectly straight walls appear to come to a point. The second corridor is dark, rough, and winding. The walls have been fashioned to resemble the walls of a cave, and the distance between them is highly irregular; sometimes they come so close together that the Emperor can barely force his way through, while at other times they are twice the distance apart of the jade walls of the straight corridor. This corridor is lit by sputtering torches that leave long spaces of blackness. The floor is earthen and littered with stones; an occasional dark puddle reflects a torch.

HOURGLASSES

The art of the hourglass is highly developed in Cathay. White sand and red sand are most common, but sands of all colors are widely used, although many prefer snow-water or quicksilver. The glass containers assume a lavish variety of forms; the monkey hourglasses of our Northeast provinces are justly renowned. Exquisite erotic hourglasses, often draped in translucent silks, are seen in the home of every nobleman. Our Emperor has a passion for hourglasses; aside from his private collection there are innumerable hourglasses throughout the vast reaches of the Imperial Palace, including the gardens and parks, so that the Turner of Hourglasses and his many assistants are continually busy. It is said that the Emperor carries with him, sewn into his robe, a tiny golden hourglass, fashioned by one of the court miniaturists. It is said that if you stand in any of the myriad halls, chambers, and corridors of the Imperial Palace, and listen intently in the silence of the night, you can hear the faint and neverending sound of sand sifting through hourglasses.

CONCUBINES

The Emperor's concubines live in secluded but splendid apartments in the Northwest Wing, where the mechanicians and miniaturists are also lodged. The proximity is not fanciful, for the concubines are honored as artificers. The walk of a concubine is a masterpiece of lubricity in comparison to which the tumultuous motions of an ordinary woman carried to rapture by the act of love are a formal expression of polite interest in a boring conversation. For an ordinary mortal to witness the walk of a concubine, even accidentally and through a distant lattice-window, is for him to experience a destructive ecstasy far in excess of the intensest pleasures he has known. These unfortunate courtiers, broken by a glance, pass the remainder of their lives in a feverish torment of unsatisfied longing. The concubines, some of whom are as young as fourteen, are said to wear four transparent silk robes, of scarlet, rose-yellow, white, and plum, respectively. What we know of their art comes to us by way of the eunuchs, who enjoy their privileged position and are not always to be trusted. That art appears to depend in large part upon the erotic paradoxes of transparent concealment and opaque revelation. Mirrors, silks, the dark velvet of rugs and coverlets, transparent blue pools in the concealed courtyard, scarves and sashes, veils, scarlet and jade light through colored glass, shadows, implications, illusions, duplicities of disclosure, a profound understanding of monotony and surprise—such are the tools of the concubines' art. Although they live in the palace, they have about them an insubstantiality, an air of legend, for they are never seen except by the Emperor, who is divine, by the attendant eunuchs, who are not real men, and by such courtiers as are half mad with tormented longing and cannot explain what they have seen. It has been said that the concubines do not exist; the jest contains a deep truth, for like all artists they live so profoundly in illusion that gradually their lives grow illusory. It is not too much to say that these high representatives of the flesh, these lavish expressions of desire, live entirely in spirit; they are abstract as scholars; they are our only virgins.

BOREDOM

Our boredom, like our zest, can only be as great as our lives. How much greater and more terrible, then, must be the boredom of our Emperor, which flows into every corridor of the palace, spills into the parks and gardens, stretches to the utmost edges of our unimaginably vast empire, and, still not exhausted, but perhaps even strengthened by such exercise, rises to the height of heaven itself.

DWARFS

The Emperor has two dwarfs, both of whom are disliked by the court, although for different reasons. One dwarf is dark, humpbacked, and coarse-featured, with long unruly hair. This dwarf mocks the Emperor, imitates his gestures in a disrespectful way, contradicts his opinions, and in general plays the buffoon. Sometimes he runs among the Court ladies, brushing against them as he passes, and even, to the horror of everyone, lifting their robes and concealing himself beneath them. Nothing is more disturbing than to see a beautiful Court lady standing with this impudent lump beneath her robe. The ladies are nevertheless forced to endure such indignities, for the Emperor has given his dwarf freedoms which no one else receives. The other dwarf is neat, aloof, and severe in feature and dress. The Emperor often discusses with him questions of philosophy, art, and warfare. This dwarf detests the dark dwarf, whom he once wounded gravely in a duel; so far as possible they avoid each other. Far from approving of the dark dwarf's rival, we are intensely jealous of his intimacy with the Emperor. If one were to ask us which dwarf is more pleasing, our unhesitating answer would be: we want them both dead.

EYELIDS

The art of illuminating the eyelid is old and honorable, and no Court lady is without her miniaturist. These delicate and precise paintings, in black, white, red, green, and blue ink, are highly prized by our courtiers, and especially by lovers, who read in them profound and ambiguous messages. One can never be certain, when one sees a handsome courtier gazing passionately into the eyes of a beautiful lady, whether he is searching for the soul behind her eyes or whether he is striving to attain a glimpse of her elegant and dangerous eyelids. These paintings are never the same, and indeed are different for each eyelid, and one cannot know, gazing across the room at a beautiful lady with whom one has not yet become intimate, whether her lowered eyelids will reveal a tall willow with dripping branches; an arched bridge in snow; a pear blossom and hummingbird; a crane among cocks; rice leaves bending in the wind; a wall with open gate, through which can be seen a distant village on a hillside. When speaking, a Court lady will lower her eyelids many times, offering tantalizing glimpses of little scenes that seem to express the elusive mystery of her soul. The lover well knows that these eyelid miniatures, at once public and intimate, half-exposed and always hiding, allude to the secret miniatures of the hidden eyes, or the eyes of the breast. These miniature masterpieces are inked upon the rosy areola surrounding the nipple and sometimes upon the sides and tip of the nipple itself. A lover disrobing his mistress in the first ecstasy of her consent is so eager for his sight of those secret miniatures that sometimes he lingers too long in rapturous contemplation and thereby incurs severe displeasure. Some Court ladies delight in erotic miniatures of the most startling kind, and it is impossible to express the troubled excitement with which a lover, stirred to exaltation by the elegant turn of a cheekbone and the shy purity of a glance, discovers upon the breast of his beloved an exquisitely inked scene of riot and debauchery.

DRAGONS

The dragons of Cathay dwell in caves in the mountains of the North and in the depths of the Eastern sea. The dragons rarely show themselves, but we are always aware of them, for their motions are responsible for storms at sea, great waves, hurricanes, tornadoes, and earthquakes. A sea dragon rising from the waves can sink an entire fleet with one lash of its terrible tail. Sometimes a northern dragon will leave its cave and fly through the air, covering whole cities with its immense shadow. Those who have stood in the shadow of the dragon say it is accompanied by an icy wind. The tail of a dragon, glittering in the light of the sun, is said to be covered with blue and yellow scales. The head of a dragon is emerald and gold, its tongue scarlet, its eyes pits of fire. It is said that the venom which drips from its terrible jaws is hotter than boiling pitch. It is said that to see a dragon is to be changed forever. Some do not believe in dragons, because they have not seen them; it is like not believing in one's own death, because one has not yet died.

MINIATURES

Our passion for the miniature is by no means exhausted by the painting of eyelids; the art of carving in miniature is one of the oldest and most esteemed of our arts. Well known is the Emperor's miniature palace, which sits upon a jade cabinet beside the tree with the twelve singing birds, and which is said to reproduce with absolute fidelity the vast Imperial Palace, with its thousands of chambers and corridors, as well as its innumerable courtyards, parks, and gardens. Within the miniature palace, which is no larger than a small table, one can see, by means of a magnifying lens, myriad pieces of precise furniture, as well as entire sets of cups, bowls, and dishes, and even a pair of scissors so tiny that when fully opened they can be concealed behind the leg of a fly. In the miniature throne room one can see a minute jade table with a miniature palace, and it is said that within this second palace, which can scarcely be seen by the naked eye, the artist has again reproduced the entire Imperial Palace.

SUMMER NIGHTS

On a summer night, when the moon is a white blossom in a blue garden, it is good to go out of the palace and walk in the Garden of Islands. The arched wooden bridges over their perfect reflections, the hanging willows, the white swans over the swans in the dark water, the yellow and blue lights in the palace, the smell of plum blossoms, all these speak of peace and harmony, and quell the rebellious restlessness of the soul. If, on such a night, one happens to see a dark-green frog leap into the water, sending out a rainbow of ripples that make the moon waver, one's happiness is complete.

UGLY WOMEN

It is well known that the Court ladies are the loveliest in the empire, but among them one always sees several who can only be called ugly. We are not speaking of ladies who are grotesque, monstrous, or unclean, but merely of ladies who are strikingly unpleasing to our eyes. Instead of thin, arched eyebrows they have thick, straight eyebrows, which sometimes grow together; one or more of their teeth may be noticeably crooked; their noses and mouths are too large, their eyes too wide apart or close together. Since no one can remain at the palace without the consent of the Emperor, it is clear that he considers their presence inoffensive, and perhaps even desirable. Indeed, to the embarrassment of the court, he has sometimes chosen an ugly lady for his mistress. It is a mystery that teases the understanding, for to say that the Emperor is an admirer of beauty is to speak with misleading coolness. Our

Emperor reveres beauty, lives and breathes in a world of beautiful objects, lavishes wealth and honor on the creators of beauty, is, despite his terrible omnipotence, entirely submissive to the beauty of a teacup, a plum blossom, a white cheek. The Empress is renowned for her delicate loveliness. How is it, then, that our Emperor can bear to have ugly women in his court, and appears even to encourage their presence? It is easy of course to imagine that he sometimes grows weary of the exquisitely beautiful women who meet his gaze wherever he turns. In the same way our court poets are advised to introduce occasional small dullnesses and imperfections into their verses, in order to relieve the hearer from the monotony of perfection. One can even go further, and grant that the beauty of our ladies has about it a high, noble, and spiritual quality that lifts it above the realm of the merely physical. But ugliness, by its very nature, draws attention to the physical. One might imagine, then, that the Emperor longs to escape from the spiritual beauty of our Court ladies and to abandon himself to the physical pleasures which seem to be promised by the ugly ladies—as if the coarseness and impropriety of their faces were an intimation or revelation of dark, coarse, improper pleasures hidden beneath their elegant silks. Yet it is difficult to see how this can be the true explanation, since the Emperor's longing for sensual pleasure may always be satisfied by his incomparable concubines. Another explanation remains. It is known that the Emperor is an admirer of beauty; there is no reason to assume that in this instance he has changed. Is it not possible that the Emperor sees in these ugly women a beauty to which we, with our smaller understanding, are hopelessly blind? Our poets have said that there can be no beauty without strangeness. One imagines our Emperor returning to his chamber from the stimulation of his concubines. From those unimaginably desirable women, those masterpieces of the art of appearance, who express in every feature of face and body the physical loveliness he has craved, he is returning to a world of Court ladies, themselves flowers of beauty who in some turn of the lip, some glance, some look of sweet pensiveness may even surpass the wholly sensual beauty of his concubines. As he passes through the corridors leading to the East Wing, he comes upon a lady and her maids. The lady has thick, straight eyebrows that nearly grow together; her nose is broad; she gives a clumsy curtsey. The ugly eyebrows, the broad nose, the clumsy gestures irritate his dulled senses into attention, and many days later, when he has passed long hours among his concubines and lovely ladies, he will suddenly recall, with a burst of excitement, those thick eyebrows, that broad nose, that clumsy curtsey, for like a beautiful woman suddenly glimpsed behind a lattice-window she will lead his soul away from the torpor of the familiar into a dark realm of strangeness and wonder.

ISLANDS

The floating islands of Cathay are most commonly found in our lakes, especially the great southern lakes, but they occur in our rivers as well. Nothing is more delightful, for a group of Court ladies walking by a pleasant riverside, than to see one of these islands floating by. The younger ladies, little more than girls, laugh and cry out, and even older and more sober women can scarcely suppress their joy. It is quite different when these same ladies are in a boat on the water, for then the island, whose motions are entirely unpredictable, is an object of great terror. Except for their motion, these islands are like ordinary islands, and the question of their origin has never been answered. Our ancient historians classified floating islands with water-animals, but we are less certain. Some believe that floating islands are a special race of islands, which reproduce and which have no relation whatever to common islands. Others believe that floating islands are common islands that have broken away; animated by boredom, melancholy, and restlessness, they follow no certain path, bringing with them the joy of surprise and the pain of the unknown.

MIRRORS

The ladies of Cathay, and above all the Court ladies, have for their mirrors a passion so intense that a lover feels he can never inspire such ardors of uninterrupted attention. The mirror of a lady holds her with its powerful and irresistible gaze, desires her to be wholly his, and in the privacy of the night encourages disrobings. What torture for the yearning and neglected lover to imagine his lady at night in her chamber, alone with her amorous mirror. He imagines the mirror's passionate and hungry gaze, which holds her spellbound; the long, searching look, deep into her treacherous eyes; her slow surrender to the act of reflection. The mirror, having drawn the lady into his silver depths, begins to yearn for still greater intimacies. Once in the glass, she begins to feel an inner tickling; she feels about to swoon; her eyes, half-closed, have a veiled and drowsy look; and all at once, yielding to her mirror's imperious need, she slips from her robe, and boldly gives her nakedness to the glass. And perhaps, when she turns her back to her mirror, in preparation for peering slyly over her shoulder, for a moment she hesitates, permitting herself to be seen and savored by the insatiable glass, feeling her skin tingle in that stern, lecherous, unsparing gaze. Is it surprising that her lover, meeting her the next morning, sees that she is pale and somewhat tired, not yet recovered from the excesses of the night?

YEARNING

There are fifty-four Steps of Love, of which the fifth is Yearning. There are seventeen degrees of yearning, through all of which the lover must pass before reaching the Sixth Step, which is Restlessness.

THE PALACE

The palace of the Emperor is so vast that a man cannot pass through all its chambers in a lifetime. Whole portions of the palace are neglected and abandoned, and begin to lead a strange, independent existence. It is told how the Emperor, riding alone one day in one of the southeastern gardens, dismounted and entered a wing of the palace through an open window. He had never seen the chambers of this wing before; their decorations had for him an inexpressible and faintly troubling charm. Coming upon an old man, dressed in old-fashioned ceremonial robes, he asked a question; the man replied in an accent which the Emperor had never heard. In time the Emperor discovered that the inhabitants of this wing were descendants of the Emperor's great-grandfather; living for four generations in this unfrequented part of the palace, they had kept to the old ways, and the old pronunciation. Shaken, the Emperor rode away, and in the ensuing nights paid many visits to his concubines.

BLUE HORSES

The Emperor's blue horses in a field of white snow.

SORROW

The Twelve Images of Sorrow are: the autumn moon behind three black branches, a mirror when it does not reflect a face, a single white plum-petal hanging from a bough, the eyes of a beautiful lady at dusk, a garden in summer rain, frosty breath on an autumn night, an old man gazing at a river, a faded fan, a dead sparrow in the snow, a lover leaving his mistress at dawn, an old abandoned hourglass, the black form of the wild duck against the red setting sun. These are the sorrows known to all men, but there is a sorrow that is only of Cathay. Our sorrow is the sorrow hidden in the depths of rich, deep-blue summer afternoons, the sorrow of sunshine on the blossoming plum tree, the sorrow that lies like a faint purple shadow in the iris of a beautiful, laughing girl.

THE MAN IN A MAZE

It sometimes happens that a child's toy, newly invented by one of the sublime toymakers of Cathay, enchants our Emperor. The toy is at once taken up by his courtiers, and for days or weeks or even months at a time the entire court is in a fever over that toy, which suddenly drops into disfavor and soon passes out of existence altogether. One such toy that took the fancy of the Emperor was a small closed ivory box, of a size easily held in the hand. The inside of the box was composed of many partitions, forming a maze. The partitions were invisible but were shown by black lines on the outside of the box. The tiny, invisible ball, which was of gold, was called The Man in a Maze. One would often see the Emperor standing alone by a window, his head bowed gravely over the little toy that he held in the palm of his hand.

BARBARIANS

Often there is talk of the barbarians who press upon us at the outermost limits of the empire. Although our armies are invincible, our fortifications impregnable, our mountains impassable, and our forests impenetrable, our women shudder and look about with uneasy eyes. Sometimes a forbidden thought comes: to be a barbarian, to sit upon a black horse with flaming nostrils and hooves of thunder, to ride swifter than fire with one's long hair streaming in the wind.

THE CONTEST OF MAGICIANS

In the shimmering and legendary past of Cathay, when history and fable were often confounded, an Emperor is said to have held a contest of magicians. From all four quarters of the empire the magicians flocked to the Imperial Palace, to perform in the throne room and seek to be chosen as Court Magician. In those days the art of magic was taken far more seriously than it is today, and scarcely a boy in the empire but could turn a peach blossom into a dove. The Emperor, seated high on his throne in the presence of his most powerful courtiers and his most beautiful Court ladies, permitted each magician only a single trick, after which the magician was informed, by means of a folded note brought to him on a silver tray outside the doors of the throne room, whether he was to depart or stay. Those chosen to remain were lodged in elegant chambers, and later were asked to perform a second time before the Emperor, although on this occasion the performance took place in the presence of two rival magicians. Since two of the three magicians were destined to be dismissed, there was a strong air of drama about this stage of the contest, and it is said that the magicians continually sought to bribe the courtiers and Court ladies, all of whom, however, remained incorruptible. Some magicians wished to be the first of the three to perform, others longed to be second, and still others believed that the advantage lay with him who was third, and many arguments raged on all three sides of the question—quite in vain, since the order was decided by lot, the rice leaves being drawn by the Empress herself. The one hundred twenty-eight magicians remaining after this stage of the battle were now requested to perform in pairs; and in this manner the magicians were gradually reduced to sixty-four, and to thirty-two, and to sixteen, and to eight, and to four, and at last to only two. When there were only two magicians left, one of whom was a vigorous man of ripe years, and the other an old man with a white beard, there was a pause for one week, during which the court prepared for the final match, while the magicians were permitted to rest or practice, as they pleased. At last the great day came, the lots were drawn, and the younger man was chosen to perform first. He had astonished everyone with the daring and elegance of his earlier performances, and a hush came over the court as he climbed the carpeted steps of the handsome ebony and ivory platform constructed for the magicians by the Emperor's own carpenter. The magician bowed, and announced that he had a request. He asked a member of the court to bring to him, there on his platform, the statue of a beautiful woman. He himself would gladly bring a jade or marble statue out of the ends of his fingers; but he asked for a statue to be brought to him so that there could be no question concerning the true nature of the statue. This unusual request produced murmurs of uncertainty, but at last it was decided to humor his whim; and six strong courtiers were dispatched to fetch from the Emperor's collection the statue of a beautiful woman. It was promptly done; and the beautiful jade statue stood upon the ebony and ivory platform. The magician moved his hands before the stone woman, and as the court watched in awe, the statue slowly began to wake. The jade body turned to flesh, the jade lips to red lips, the jade hair to shiny black hair; and a beautiful living girl stood on the platform, looking about in bewilderment. The magician at once robed her, and led her forth among the astonished court; she spoke, and laughed, and in every way was a real, live girl. So awestruck were the courtiers, who had never seen any trick like it before, that they almost forgot the second magician, who sat to one side and waited. After a while the attention of the court returned to the neglected magician, about whom they were now curious, for no one could imagine a more brilliant trick than the godlike deed of breathing life into inanimate matter. The old magician, who was by no means feeble, took his place on the platform, and to the surprise of all present he praised his rival, saying that in all his years of devotion to the noble art of magic he had seen nothing to equal such a deed. For certainly it was wonderful to bring life out of stone, just as in the ancient fables. He hoped, too, that a woman of such high beauty would not frown upon the praises of an old magician. At this the newly created woman smiled, and looked all the more beautiful. The old magician then bowed, and said that he too had a request: he would like the six courtiers to bring him the statue of a beautiful woman. The court was surprised at the old magician's request, for even if he had mastered the art of bringing forth a live woman from the stone, his deed could only equal that of his rival, without surpassing it; and by virtue of being second, he would seem only an imitator, without daring or originality. Meanwhile the six courtiers fetched a second jade statue, and placed it upon the ebony and ivory platform. In beauty the second statue rivaled the first, and young courtiers crowded close to the platform, eagerly awaiting her transformation. The old magician waved his hands before the stone, and slowly it began to wake. The jade arms moved, the jade lips parted, the jade eyes blinked and looked about; and a beautiful jade girl stood on the platform, smiling and crossing her smooth jade arms. The magician led her forth among the marveling courtiers, who reached out to touch her green arms and her green hair; and some said her arms were jade, yet warm, and some said her arms were flesh, but stony cold. All crowded around her, staring and wondering; and the old magician led her up to the Emperor. His Imperial Majesty said that although there were many beautiful women in his court, there was but one breathing statue; and without hesitation he awarded the prize to the old magician. It is said that the first woman grew ill-tempered at the attention showered upon her rival, and that the first task of the new Court Magician was to change her back into a beautiful statue.

A NOTE ABOUT THE AUTHOR

Steven Millhauser was born in 1943 in New York City and grew up in Connecticut. He is the author of *Edwin Mullhouse: The Life and Death of an American Writer,* which won the Prix Médicis Etranger, and *Portrait of a Romantic.* His stories have been published in *The New Yorker, Antaeus, Grand Street, The Hudson Review,* and other periodicals. He lives with his wife in Mamaroneck, New York.

A NOTE ON THE TYPE

This book was set in a digitized version of a type face called Baskerville. The face itself is a facsimile reproduction of types cast from molds made for John Baskerville (1706–1775) from his designs. Baskerville's original face was one of the forerunners of the type style known to printers as "modern face"—a "modern" of the period A.D. 1800.

Composed by The Brevis Press, Bethany, Connecticut.
Printed and bound by The Haddon Craftsmen, Inc.,
Scranton, Pennsylvania.

Designed by Virginia Tan.